RENA GEORGE

A
CORNISH
OBSESSION

Complete and Unabridged

LINFORD
Leicester

First published in Great Britain in 2014

First Linford Edition
published 2016

A catalogue record for this book is available
from the British Library.

ISBN 978–1–4448–2770–5

Published by
F. A. Thorpe (Publishing)
Anstey, Leicestershire

Set by Words & Graphics Ltd.
Anstey, Leicestershire
Printed and bound in Great Britain by
T. J. International Ltd., Padstow, Cornwall

This book is printed on acid-free paper

A CORNISH OBSESSION

It's a snowy December night in Marazion, and Jago Tilley is making his unsteady way home from the village pub. By morning, he will be dead . . . Investigating the brutal murder is DI Sam Kitto — and, once again, his magazine editor girlfriend Loveday Ross finds herself involved in the case. Suspicion falls on several people — the dead man's disreputable nephew; an arrogant art dealer; and a glamorous boutique owner. Meanwhile, Loveday's boss is acting distinctly out of character . . .

1

It had snowed during the night, leaving a thin white covering over rooftops, streets, and gardens. Loveday sighed, and glanced up at the depressingly dark sky. It wasn't a morning for jogging along the beach, but she had to get away from the cottage, from the memory of the previous evening's ugly exchanges between her and Sam.

She hadn't meant for them to split up, not really. But Sam had taken it all the wrong way.

She pulled the black leather jerkin over her tracksuit and zipped it up to her chin before heading up the drive, leaving footprints in the snow as she crossed the road to the beach.

Anyone who saw her pounding along the tideline this morning would think she was mad — which was exactly what she was. Good and mad!

Who did Sam Kitto think he was, speaking to her like that? It was an

1

impossible relationship. She'd thought they were having a calm, adult exchange of views, but Sam hadn't reacted at all as she had expected.

'Stop seeing each other?' He'd stared at her, eyes narrowed in disbelief. 'What are you talking about?'

Loveday paced her tiny sitting-room; anything to avoid those accusing brown eyes. 'I'm not saying we can't still be friends . . . ' she'd started.

Sam put up a hand. 'Let me get this right. This is because I told you to stay out of police business, right?' He let out an exasperated sigh. 'For God's sake, Loveday. You're an intelligent woman. You must see how awkward things are for me when you go poking around my cases. The top brass already think I'm passing information to you.'

'Well, it's awkward for me too,' she said, moving to the window. There was snow in the air; she could almost smell it. Across the bay, the lights on St Michael's Mount twinkled, little pinpricks of sparkle in the darkness. She spun round to face him again. 'Everyone at the magazine assumes you tell me things, and that I'm just being coy denying it.'

'Merrick knows me better than that,' Sam snapped.

'It's not personal, you know that,' she came back, hesitating, searching for the right words. The last thing she'd intended was to hurt him, but he was taking all this the wrong way. All she wanted was a cooling-off period, a backing-off from the ever-increasing rows. She crossed the room and took his hand. 'I just think we need some time away from each other,' she said gently.

But he'd snatched his hand away, his eyes darkening in anger. What was she doing? It was all coming out wrong. She'd been about to tell him she was thinking of going home to Scotland for Christmas so he could spend time with his two children in Plymouth.

A breathing space for both of them, that was all she'd meant.

'I don't think there's much point in continuing this conversation,' Sam had said, getting to his feet. 'It's clear you want me to go.'

3

'But I don't,' Loveday ached to say. She wanted to put her arms around him and tell him she was sorry for starting this stupid conversation, but he was being deliberately stubborn. She stepped back as he strode past, making no effort to touch her.

'Sam . . . ' she started, as he ducked through the low door. But he didn't turn. She could sense the willpower he was mustering not to slam the door behind him as he stormed out.

But that was last night and she had to stop thinking about it. She took a deep breath, focusing on pacing herself as she followed the curve of the beach.

By the time she got back to her cottage she was panting. She could hear her mobile phone ringing on the other side of the kitchen door. It was bound to be Sam. Did she even want to talk to him? She wasn't sure. But when she got in and reached for it, she saw Cassie's name.

'Please tell me you're not ringing me from next door, Cassie?'

There was a slight pause, and then her friend said, 'What's got into you today?

4

Get out of bed on the wrong side, did we?'

Loveday flopped into a chair. 'I'm sorry, ignore me . . . just got in from my run and I'm still all over the place.'

'I thought that was supposed to chill you out?'

'Yeah,' Loveday said wearily, pushing a hand through her long dark hair. 'But not till after my shower.'

'Well, okay,' Cassie said. 'But after that . . . have you anything planned?'

'Other than pigging out on chocolate, and watching an old black-and-white movie on TV? No, not really.'

'Fancy a spot of baking?'

'What?'

'Yes, you heard. I've been roped into doing the food for the sailing club's Christmas do. I'd be grateful for another pair of hands. What d'you think?'

Loveday sighed. 'You do know that my sponge puddings have been used to cement cracks in pavements?'

Cassie laughed. 'Yes, I did hear that, but I'm willing to risk it if you are.'

There was a moment's hesitation and

then Loveday said, 'When you put it as nicely as that, how can I refuse?'

'Come by when you're ready then. And Loveday . . . thanks.'

It took ten minutes to shower, then another five to get into her jeans and sweater, and plait her hair into a tidy long rope.

Delicious baking smells were already wafting from Cassie's kitchen as Loveday crossed the yard and tapped the door before walking in. She glanced around.

The big, bright room looked under siege. A heap of messy plates, cups, mixing bowls and spoons filled one of the two sinks. The big wooden table was littered with baking paraphernalia, and on the worktop next to the Aga were several trays of pastries and fairy cakes.

Cassie looked up and pushed her long blonde fringe out of her eyes with the heel of a floury hand. 'I know,' she grinned. 'It's like organized chaos.'

Loveday raised an eyebrow. 'What have you done with the kids?'

'Well, I haven't strangled them or anything, although it has been tempting.'

6

She nodded towards the door. 'They're watching children's telly in the front room. Adam's got his Saturday surgery this morning, so they've been warned to be quiet.'

Loveday gave her a wistful smile. 'Sophie and Leo are great kids. You two are so lucky.'

Cassie looked up from her mixing bowl. 'That came from the heart.' She searched her friend's face. 'Okay, what's up?'

Loveday gave a weary sigh. 'Just me putting my big foot in everything . . . *again.*'

Cassie waited.

'Sam and I have split up.'

Her friend's eyes widened. 'Ah . . . '

Loveday looked away, hoping Cassie had missed the prick of tears in her eyes.

'It was me who finished it,' she said quickly. 'I didn't mean to. I just needed some space. Sam's on duty over most of the holidays and I was thinking of going up to Scotland to spend Christmas with my family. It all seemed like such a good idea yesterday.'

'I take it Sam didn't see it that way?'

Loveday shook her head. 'He thinks I don't want him, but it's not that.'

'What then?'

'Oh, I don't know, Cassie. I just wish now that I'd left well alone.'

'Would coffee help?' Her friend smiled.

Loveday's nose was twitching. 'Can you smell burning?'

Cassie rushed across the kitchen and threw open the oven door. A cloud of black smoke filled the room. The smoke detector in the hall began to buzz noisily. Sophie and Leo charged in, and from the far side of the house Adam's feet could be heard pounding towards them.

'It's fine,' she called out, hands raised in a 'stay calm' gesture as he appeared at the kitchen door. 'Just some cremated mince pies.'

Adam shook his head, grinning. 'I'll get back and reassure my patients that we're not evacuating the building, then.'

'Sorry, darling!' Cassie grimaced after him as he returned to his surgery, turning off the smoke detector as he passed it.

'Will the fire engines be coming, Mummy?' Leo asked excitedly.

'Not this time, angel.' Cassie ruffled Leo's blond hair. 'It was a false alarm. You two go back to the front room and I'll bring in some juice and biscuits.'

Both children looked so disappointed that there was to be no fire and rescue drama that Loveday threw her arms around them, promising to bring the snacks through herself.

She was still smiling after them when the hammering started on the kitchen door.

Cassie glanced up, frowning, but before she could wipe her hands, the door flew open and a small, elderly woman rushed in.

Cassie's eyes widened in surprise. 'Priddy! Whatever's happened?' In an instant she was across the room, an arm around the old lady's shoulders, guiding her to a chair.

Loveday took a glass from the drainer and filled it from the tap.

'Here,' she said gently, handing it to the agitated visitor. 'Sip this.'

The woman accepted the glass and took a sip of water before handing it back.

'It's all right, Priddy,' Cassie said soothingly. 'Take your time. Just tell us what on earth has happened.'

The woman's face crumpled as she burst into sobs.

'It's Jago,' she cried shakily. 'I . . . I think he's dead.'

'Dead?' Cassie repeated, glancing up at Loveday.

Priddy nodded, a saturated hankie balled into her fist. She was trying to control the sobbing.

'I came to fetch the doctor . . . I need him to come back with me.'

Loveday touched the old lady's shoulder.

'Try to stay calm,' she said gently. 'Can you tell us what happened?'

The frightened blue eyes stared up at her.

'It was that old stair carpet . . . I told him this would happen, but he wouldn't listen.' Priddy bit her lip and reached out for Cassie's hand. And then she noticed the table strewn with baking things. 'That's what I was doing this morning, too. I always pop a few scones through to

Jago on a Saturday morning.' She gave a tearful smile. 'He's partial to a fruit scone, is Jago. But this time he didn't answer my knock, so I tried the door handle. It wasn't locked. He always keeps it locked.' The worried eyes filled with tears again, and the voice came out in juddering gasps. 'He was on the floor . . . at the bottom of the stairs . . . just lying there like some poor broken doll.'

Cassie glanced again at Loveday.

'Could you fetch Adam?'

Loveday nodded and hurried through the house to Adam's surgery, making her apologies to the surprised patients in the waiting room. She rapped on the surgery door.

'Come in,' Adam called, after a moment.

Loveday stuck her head round the door.

'Sorry to interrupt, but I think this might be important.'

Adam finished signing his patient's prescription and handed it to him. The man got up, giving Loveday a curious look as he left.

She waited until they were alone before

hurriedly repeating Priddy's story.

Adam followed her back to the kitchen, crouching in front of Priddy and taking her hand. The woman was one of his patients, and he knew her history of high blood pressure. He spoke quietly, but Priddy interrupted.

'I didn't know what to do, doctor,' she sniffed. 'I think he's dead. Will you come back with me?'

Adam patted her hand.

'Of course I will. I'll just get my bag.'

Cassie's face had turned as white as her flour, and Loveday touched her arm.

'I think you should sit down. You've had a shock too.'

Cassie was shaking her head. 'Poor Jago.' Her eyes were on the old lady. 'I am so sorry, Priddy.'

Adam returned as quickly as he'd left, having hurriedly explained to his waiting patients that he had to attend an emergency.

'I think you should stay here with Cassie,' he told Priddy as he crossed to the door.

But Priddy sprang to her feet.

'I'm coming with you.'

Cassie looked across at Loveday.

'Maybe you should go with them.'

'Of course,' Loveday said.

There was no time for conversation as the three of them hurried along the road. Loveday had never actually spoken to Priddy before, but she'd seen her about the village and knew she lived in one of the cottages that overlooked the beach.

Adam was striking out ahead of them and Loveday held back, keeping pace with Priddy's slower step. Her heart went out to the old lady. Judging by her distress it was obvious that she and Jago Tilley had been close.

The three of them drew curious looks as they hurried past the hotel. A tall, glittering Christmas tree was visible through the glass doors. The post office and the village store were also festooned with seasonal cheer, and fairy lights were strung around the small town square.

Everyone they passed seemed to know Priddy, and several people tried to stop her, asking what was wrong, but Priddy shook her head at each one.

'I can't stop now . . .'

Loveday was aware of the stares that followed them along the road. If Jago Tilley really was dead, the whole of Marazion would know about it soon enough.

Just past the square, Adam turned right into the terrace of four cottages. The first two had an unoccupied look. Adam stopped at the next one, and Loveday took in the dilapidated appearance. The little house was in serious need of care and attention. It stood out in stark contrast to the pristine condition of the adjoining cottage, which Loveday presumed was Priddy's home.

Adam went into Jago's place. Loveday's first instinct was to follow him in, but she held back. Priddy was already distressed enough. There was no need for her to face that trauma all over again. They would know soon enough if the man really was dead.

'I think we should wait in your cottage,' she suggested, trying to lead her away from Jago's front door.

But Priddy had other ideas. 'I have to

know . . . I have to know if Jago is . . . '

She was rushing through after Adam, Loveday at her heels. They both stopped as they entered the hall. Even to Loveday's inexperienced eye it was obvious the poor man was dead.

Adam put up his hand to stop them advancing further. His eyes slid to the top of the stairs, where Loveday could see the carpet was quite obviously ruffled.

'I think you should call Sam, Loveday.'

Loveday stared at him, and then back up the stairs. What had she missed? Surely this was a straightforward accident? And then she saw it . . . very faint scratches on the wall, and traces of what could be blood.

Adam's eyes were grave.

'Call Sam,' he repeated.

Loveday didn't wait to question him. She slipped out, reaching into her pocket for her phone and clicked on Sam's number.

He answered instantly, as though he had been waiting for her call.

'Sam?'

At the sound of her voice Sam's heart

15

did an annoying little flip.

'Loveday?'

Was that hope in his voice? Loveday wondered. As if she didn't feel bad enough already. She launched straight in.

'Adam thinks you should come down here, Sam.' She glanced back to make sure Priddy wasn't in earshot. 'There's been a sudden death.' She hesitated before going on. 'And Adam's not happy about it.'

'Where are you?'

Sam's voice had snapped into professional mode.

Loveday told him.

'I'll see you both there,' he said briskly, and the phone clicked off.

Adam and Priddy were emerging from Jago's cottage as Loveday turned back.

'Priddy is going to make us all a nice cup of tea,' he said, narrowing his eyes at Loveday. She understood the unspoken question and nodded, confirming that Sam was on his way.

2

Storm Cottage was at the beach end of the terrace and had a direct view over the bay. Seeing it now, Loveday realized she passed it almost every day when she jogged along the front. She remembered the stone steps that curved up from the shingle to a little iron gate, and a garden beyond. She'd often wondered who lived here, but this wasn't the way she'd wanted to find out.

The kitchen was larger than Loveday had imagined for such a small cottage, but not big enough for it to have lost its cosiness. The embers of a log fire, abandoned when Priddy had rushed out to find Adam, still glowed in an old black range; a collection of colourful Christmas cards jostled for space on the mantelshelf above.

There were no modern kitchen units, but the shelves of an old pine dresser, that looked as if it had stood in the same spot since the cottage was built, were filled with blue and white china. A tiny Christmas tree, sparkling with multi-coloured fairy lights, cast a cheerful glow over the scene.

'Shift yourself, Muffin.' Priddy shooed an enormous black cat off the armchair and sank wearily down onto it.

Loveday took a seat by the table, but Adam remained standing by the window, from where he had a view of the terrace.

The old lady stared into the fire.

'I warned him about that stair carpet.' She shook her head. 'But you couldn't tell Jago anything. He always knew best.' She looked up at Adam. 'I mean . . . how much would a new carpet have cost him? It wasn't as though he couldn't afford it.'

She caught the look that passed between Adam and Loveday, and her expression changed to one of concern.

'He did fall down the stairs, didn't he? I mean . . . it was an accident?'

Loveday got up and put an arm around Priddy's shoulders.

'We don't know yet how it happened.' She hesitated, glancing at Adam. 'But it's

18

always best to make sure, which is why Dr Trevillick thought we should call the police.'

Priddy's china-blue eyes stared back at her. 'The police?' Her gaze moved from one to the other, finally settling on Adam. 'So you don't think it was an accident? You think someone . . . ' She gulped. 'You think someone pushed Jago down those stairs.'

Loveday patted her shoulder.

'I think we could all do with that cup of tea.' She felt the woman stir to struggle up, and put more pressure on her shoulders. 'No, you just sit there, Priddy. I'll do it.'

Loveday busied herself with the tea things as Priddy's expression switched from grief to confusion. She looked at Adam.

'Who would do such a terrible thing, Dr Trevillick? Jago could be a cantankerous old devil sometimes, but he was a good man.'

Adam tried a reassuring smile.

'We don't know anything yet, Priddy.'

But the old lady's brow furrowed as her

19

mind scrolled through the possibilities. She shook her head.

'No ... I don't believe it. The old devil's got himself drunk and missed his footing, and he's come crashing down those stairs. That's what must have happened.'

Loveday poured the tea and carried a cup to Priddy, who was staring into the fire again.

'He shouldn't be left through there on his own,' she said, starting to struggle to her feet. But Adam put a hand on her shoulder.

'You're right. Someone should stay with Jago. I'll go.'

It was another ten minutes before they heard Sam's car turn into the terrace. Loveday saw him stepping out, his expression grim, and watched as the passenger door also flew open and Detective Constable Amanda Fox emerged. Her mass of unruly ginger curls bobbed as she hurried after Sam. Even though it was the weekend she wore a smart navy suit over a pale blue blouse. Her skirt was a fashionable two inches above the knee and her elegant

20

matching court shoes looked new, if totally unsuitable for the snowy conditions.

Loveday glanced down at her jeans and thick white woollen pullover, and grimaced as Sam and Amanda disappeared through the open door of Jago's cottage. It was irritating how the woman always managed to make her feel dowdy. Not that she was caring too much about that at this particular moment. Her appearance was the last thing on her mind. An old man lay dead barely a few yards away.

Priddy's voice jolted her back to the present.

'That'll be the police,' the woman said numbly.

Loveday could see the tears welling up again, and her heart went out to the old lady. She pulled up a chair and sat beside her, taking her hand.

'You must have known Mr Tilley well.' She didn't know if it was the right thing to say, but she had a feeling that Priddy wanted to talk about her friend.

The blue eyes drifted back to the fire.

'Seems like forever,' she murmured. 'Jago was born in that cottage, and my

Davy was born in this one. I came here as a bride more'n forty years ago.'

'Did Jago live alone?' Loveday asked quietly.

Priddy nodded.

'No woman would have him . . . that's what he used to say. But I reckon that's the way he liked it. He could come and go as he pleased, and nobody to tell him any different.'

'Did he have no family at all?'

Priddy suddenly jumped to her feet.

'Billy! Somebody should tell Billy.'

'Who's Billy?'

'Billy Travis.' Her lips pressed into a disapproving line. 'The police will have no bother finding that one.'

Loveday was surprised.

'You mean he has a criminal record?'

'Several, I should think. He's Jago's nephew, not that Jago was ever keen to admit that, and no wonder. Billy is a right bad lot. He only ever went to see Jago when he was on the scrounge.' She shook her head. 'Jago didn't deserve family like that, but family he is, and I suppose he will have to know.'

'So Jago wasn't an only child?'

Priddy sniffed. 'Might as well have been for all the good that sister Kendra ever was to him. She was a good bit younger than Jago, but a wild one, and that's for sure.'

Loveday waited, hoping her silence would encourage the woman to continue.

Priddy nodded in the direction of Newlyn. 'Spent all her time over there, she did. All the fishermen knew her.' She leaned forward, lowering her voice conspiratorially. 'If you know what I mean.'

Loveday did. She said, 'I take it this Kendra was not married to Billy's father?'

Priddy shook her head and let out a long, heartfelt sigh. 'Thank God Maria wasn't alive to witness her daughter's shenanigans.

'When Kendra realized she was pregnant she tried to get rid of the child, and when that failed she took to the road. We heard she'd joined up with some travelling folks.'

She sighed again. 'It was twenty years later before Billy turned up in the village telling everyone his mother had died of pneumonia. Jago offered to take him in, but he'd got himself an old caravan somewhere up the hill.'

Loveday nodded.

'Well, I'm sure the police will find him.'

'Aye, and when they do, I reckon it will take no longer than an hour for him to come sniffing around here to see what he can pick up.'

Thoughts of the wayward Billy had fired Priddy with new spark, and Loveday suspected she would be a tough adversary to cross. She went on, 'If this man is Mr Tilley's only relative, then I suppose he will inherit the house.'

Priddy's eyes rounded with indignation.

'Jago wasn't that daft.'

'You mean he made a will?'

'He did indeed — and took me into Penzance with him to witness it.'

'So you know who inherits?'

Priddy nodded.

'The Newlyn Fishermen's Federation. He said all along that's what he would do, given that he, and his father before him, were fishermen.' Her eyes misted over

24

again. 'They worked an old-fashioned Cornish fishing boat out of Newlyn.' She smiled, remembering. '*Maria*, they called it, after Jago's mother. The boat was sold years ago, when it got too much for Jago on his own, but the cottage should be worth something.'

'Does Billy know about this?' Loveday asked.

Priddy's blue eyes twinkled.

'Not yet.'

Loveday's purpose in keeping Priddy talking was to divert her attention from the vehicles that were arriving outside. A big green BMW, which she recognized as belonging to Dr Robert Bartholomew, the Home Office pathologist, had just drawn up.

The white van that brought the Scene of Crime team was already in place. Their early arrival was always a priority. Loveday knew that Sam wouldn't want too many feet tramping through a possible crime scene before these people concluded their work.

There had been no sign yet of the undertaker's discreet black vehicle, so

Jago's body would still be lying next door at the foot of his stairs.

A shudder swept through Loveday as she recalled the sight, but she forced herself to fix the scene in her head. The body had been sprawled face-up on the frayed carpet at the foot of the stairs, the head on its right side, in a pool of congealed blood from a nasty-looking gash on the man's forehead. His right arm was flung out, as though he'd made a desperate attempt to save himself, and his left one was crumpled beneath him. The man's right leg was bent, while the other was stretched out, the toe of his shoed foot still on the bottom tread.

Loveday had glimpsed, through the open door directly to her right, a gloomy little sitting-room. The only item of furniture visible was the corner of what looked like a very large upholstered grey armchair. The cottage was a world away from the cheerful place next door.

There had been a sickly smell too, she remembered, and wondered how long the old man had lain there.

* * *

The initial stab of pleasure when Loveday's name flashed up on Sam's mobile phone hadn't lasted long. His first thought was that she was calling to apologize. He hadn't known what the row was about in the first place. He'd thought they were good together . . . close, even. How wrong could he have been?

As soon as she spoke he realized something was wrong.

It had been a quiet Saturday so he'd sent two of his team, DS Will Tregellis and DC Malcolm Carter, out on routine investigations; but he could see Amanda Fox's curly ginger hair bent over a file on her desk. Colleagues had nicknamed the feisty detective 'Foxy'. It wasn't a name Sam had ever used.

'We have a call-out,' he said brusquely, striding past her desk. 'A sudden death, but the local GP believes it could be suspicious.'

Amanda grabbed her jacket from the back of her chair, slipping it on as she hurried after him.

'Want me to drive, sir?' she called as they reached the car park.

Sam had been at the mercy of his young DC's erratic driving skills before. He already had his keys out.

'I'll drive,' he said.

'Where are we going, sir?' she asked as they pulled out into the busy Truro traffic.

'Marazion.'

He could feel her eyes on him. Did the whole force know about his relationship with Loveday? His expression was stern as he kept his eyes on the road.

The cottage he'd been directed to was the third one in a small terrace that ended in a cul-de-sac, high above the beach.

Sam had expected to see Adam's car, or perhaps Loveday's, but there were no vehicles — which was probably a blessing, given how narrow the terrace was.

Adam was waiting by the open front door, looking worried.

'I hope I haven't got you here on a wild goose chase,' he said.

Sam put a hand on his back, in a gesture that said, 'Better safe than sorry'.

'Where's the body?'

Adam pushed the door and it creaked as the body was revealed. The sight and smell of the congealed blood that had oozed from the victim's head made him want to retch, and he quickly glanced away. No matter how many times he'd seen similar sights, he'd never get used to this part of police work.

Sam's gaze travelled up the stairs. He knew Adam would wait before pointing out the thing that had sparked his suspicion. He would want Sam to see it for himself . . . want that confirmation that he hadn't been jumping to wrong conclusions.

The grubby stair carpet had seen better days, but it still bore traces of the floral thing it had once been. It was threadbare in patches, the canvas backing showing through, and it was ruched all the way down. It would have been easy enough for a man to catch his toe and go tumbling down the stairs — even a man who knew these stairs well.

His eyes lingered on the scratches on the landing wall, and the dark smears beside them, which could very well be blood. He longed to go up and examine the area more closely, but knew he would have to content himself until the Scene of Crime officers arrived and did their work. Despite his impatience, he didn't want to venture further and risk contaminating anything.

Sam turned to Amanda.

'Get the team here, ASAP.'

The detective, pleased that at last she had something positive to do, stepped back into the terrace, her phone already at her ear.

Sam turned to Adam. 'It was a good call. You did right to contact us.'

Adam was shaking his head.

'Poor Jago. He was one of the village characters.'

'You knew him well?'

They had stepped outside.

'Not so well as Priddy,' Adam said, indicating the immaculate cottage next door. 'She found him. Loveday is with her now.'

Sam's heart made an unbidden flip at the mention of Loveday's name. He knew he would have to see her. He wasn't sure how he felt about that. He was still confused . . . angry with her, and here she was again, right in the middle of what looked like it could be another murder.

'Do you need me any more, Sam?' Adam checked his watch. 'I left a waiting-room full of patients back at the house.'

Sam forced his mind back to the moment.

'No, of course not. You go, Adam . . . and thank you.'

The GP had already picked up his bag, and raised his hand in a backward wave as he strode up to the main road.

Sam smiled after him. Adam's wife, Cassie, was Loveday's best friend. They'd been through a few hair-raising experiences together since Loveday's arrival in Cornwall three years ago. He tried not to think about how easily Loveday seemed able to get herself into trouble.

He watched Adam's back until he'd disappeared round the corner.

In the summer months this area around the square, where the town's three hostelries and shops were clustered, would be buzzing with tourists. And there would be a steady crocodile of people making their way from the car parks at the far end of the village to the Mount. But this was December — only two short weeks until Christmas — and the locals had Marazion back to themselves.

3

It was twenty minutes before the rest of the team arrived. After he'd briefed them, and instructed Amanda to stay put outside the cottage, he slipped next door to interview the woman who'd found the body.

'Right, boss,' Amanda called after him as he marched past her.

It was Loveday who answered his light tap.

'Hello, Sam.' She stood aside awkwardly to let him pass.

He felt a brief surge of satisfaction at her apparent unease. He caught her arm as she turned to lead the way into Priddy's kitchen.

'What exactly are you doing here?'

Loveday thought about being annoyed at his brusque tone, then decided life was too short — and she was beginning to feel she had already behaved quite badly enough to him.

She swallowed, keeping her voice low

so that Priddy would not hear.

'I was with Cassie when Priddy came to find Adam. The poor woman was in a terrible state. She told us she thought her neighbour was dead. I came back with her and Adam because I thought I could help.'

Sam nodded. That sounded reasonable enough. He cleared his throat and conceded, 'I'm sure you have helped.'

They moved into the kitchen. It smelled faintly of baking — a comforting, homely smell. Sam's ex-wife, Victoria, used to bake in the early days of their marriage. It made him think of his children, and felt a sudden surge of sadness. Jack and Maddie were aged twelve and nine now, and they were growing up without him. Today was Saturday. Would Victoria be taking them out somewhere? Would her new man be accompanying them? He was immediately angry with himself for even considering it. He snapped his mind back to professional mode.

'Priddy, this is Detective Inspector Kitto.' Loveday looked at Sam. 'This is Mrs Rodda.'

'Priddy,' the old lady informed him nervously. 'Everyone just calls me Priddy.'

'Would you like me to leave, Inspector?' Loveday asked, knowing he probably would.

But Priddy chimed in anyway.

'No . . . please. I want Loveday to stay.'

Loveday glanced at Sam. He shrugged. 'I have no objection.'

He accepted Priddy's invitation to sit, and gave her a reassuring smile.

'Can you tell me what happened?' he asked gently.

Priddy gave a shuddering sigh, and retold her story.

Sam listened, letting the words form pictures in his mind.

'What about last night, Mrs Rodda . . . Priddy? Did you hear anything . . . any noises from next door?'

'Not a thing.' The old lady shook her head. 'These cottages were put up in the days when they knew how to build proper homes. If Jago had a brass band playing in his front room I wouldn't have heard a peep through these thick walls.'

Sam and Loveday exchanged a smile.

'I did hear him come home, though.'

Sam's head snapped up.

'Can you remember what time that was?'

'What time does the pub close?' Her keen eyes searched the ceiling as though she could see a replay of the previous evening's events there.

'I was in bed when I heard Muffin crying below my window. I got up to let her in. Well, I can't leave her out in this weather. She's much too old to stand the cold.'

'And did you see Mr Tilley?' Sam persisted.

'No, it was the back door I opened for Muffin. But I heard Jago messing about with his keys as I passed the front door on my way back to bed.'

'You heard him?'

'I heard his keys rattling and knew he was fumbling to open his front door.' She smiled. 'I could hear him cursing.'

'Was he alone?' Sam asked.

'I'd say so. At least, I didn't hear any other voice, and I did wait until he was inside his cottage, and the door had banged shut after him, before I went back to bed.' She looked up at Sam. 'I usually listen for him. Sometimes he couldn't find his keys and would need a hand.'

Just then, Loveday's phone rang; apologizing for the interruption, she stepped out into the hall to answer it.

'How is Priddy bearing up?' Cassie asked.

'I think she's coping,' Loveday said.

'I came down to see her, but the police have got the whole terrace taped off and they won't let me pass.'

Loveday went to the door, and was surprised to see how much more police activity was now going on outside. She could see Cassie waving to her from the other side of the blue-and-white tape, and waved back.

'Sam's here with Priddy now, Cassie. I'll ask him to give them permission to let you come down.'

She could see her friend nodding. Loveday went back and popped her head round the kitchen door.

'Could I have a word?' she asked when Sam looked up.

His brow wrinkled and he stood up, asking Priddy to excuse him.

'What's up, Loveday?'

'It's Cassie. She wants to come down to see Priddy, but your officers won't let her past the tapes.'

He fished his phone out of his pocket.

'I'll tell them to let her through.'

Loveday went back into the kitchen.

'Cassie's just outside. Is it all right if she looks in, Priddy?'

The china-blue eyes lit up for a second.

'That's good of her.' She sighed. 'I seem to be causing so many people a lot of trouble.'

Loveday reached down and squeezed her hand.

'Of course you're not. You've had a terrible shock and we all want to help.'

A young PC escorted Cassie to the front door, which Loveday had left on the latch. She came in, her face full of concern. She glanced at Sam.

'I'm sorry. Am I interrupting . . . ?'

'No, it's fine,' Sam said, turning to Priddy. 'We've finished our little chat for the moment, but we will need a proper interview with you later, if that's all right.'

'Will I have to go into the police station in Truro?' Priddy looked worried.

Sam smiled at her.

'I don't think that will be necessary. We know where to find you. But perhaps we can contact a member of your family. It might be best if you don't stay here alone tonight.'

'I suppose you could call my daughter, Jane,' Priddy said reluctantly, pointing to the writing pad by the phone. 'Her number's in there.'

'I'll ring her myself,' Sam said, going to the pad and scribbling down the information before nodding round the room and excusing himself.

'I'll stay with Priddy for a bit if you have to get off,' Cassie whispered to Loveday.

Loveday turned to Priddy.

'If you need me for anything — and I mean anything — you know where to find me. If I'm not at home, then Cassie knows how to get in touch with me.'

Priddy nodded her thanks.

The previously peaceful terrace was

now a busy thoroughfare, with police vehicles, uniformed officers, and people in white paper suits milling about. In the middle of the melee, Loveday could see the diminutive figure of DC Amanda Fox directing operations.

A curious crowd had gathered on the other side of the tape. They would know Jago was dead — news travelled fast in Cornwall — but they might not be aware of the circumstances.

'Looks like a full-scale murder investigation,' Loveday said, looking up at Sam.

'We won't know that until after the post-mortem. All this is still precautionary.' He glanced into Jago's cottage. 'Dr Bartholomew's still in there. I'll have to go and have a word with him.'

Loveday nodded. The initial awkwardness between them had gone. It was almost as if the previous evening's scene in her cottage had never happened — almost, but not quite. Loveday knew it was something that would lie at the back of both their minds until they addressed the issues. But that was for later. The drama unfolding around them was the present.

'You did a good job back there with the old lady,' Sam said unexpectedly.

Loveday looked up at him.

'Was that a compliment, Inspector?'

'If that's how you like to see it.'

'You didn't think I was . . . interfering, then?'

The barbed comment was out before she could stop it.

She saw his eyes narrow slightly.

'Quit while you're winning, Loveday,' he said stiffly.

Loveday's head was full of questions as she strolled back home. They hadn't made any arrangements to meet up later, but she knew he would call her. She had been one of the first on the scene, after all. But she hoped that wouldn't be the only reason.

Lights blazed from all the downstairs windows of Cassie and Adam's house, and Loveday could hear the children's voices. They were playing some kind of music game.

Her own little cottage was in darkness. It looked lonely and kind of sad, compared to the hilarity from next door.

She sighed. So much had happened since Sam left last night. The place felt empty without him. She had ended their relationship, and now wasn't at all sure she had done the right thing.

And then poor Jago Tilley had died — a death that was looking more like murder with every passing hour.

She unlocked the back door and let herself into the kitchen. She didn't bother switching on the light, but sank into a chair by the table, and sat in the growing dark. The sound of the children's laughter was still drifting through from next door.

She had a lot of thinking to do. Loveday had always prized her independence. Being brought up in the noisy rough-and-tumble of a boisterous, if loving, big family made having her own space extra-special now. But right at that moment she longed to be back in Scotland, helping out behind the bar of her parents' pub.

Her mobile rang, and she realized she was still sitting in the dark. She got up, reaching for the light switch as she answered the call. It was Keri.

'Just wondered if you fancied coming

over for supper tonight?'

Keri was Loveday's PA at *Cornish Folk*, the Truro-based magazine where she editor.

The mention of food made her remember she hadn't eaten all day.

'Yes, thanks, Keri. Why not? I would love that.'

'Bring Sam with you,' Keri added.

Loveday hesitated. 'Eh . . . no. It will just be me. Sam's busy.'

'Oh . . . well, okay . . . if you're sure. We're eating about seven, but come when you're ready.'

Loveday put the phone down, feeling distinctly more positive about her evening.

Keri had joined the *Cornish Folk* staff to do mainly office duties, but it had soon become obvious that her journalistic skills were as promising as her secretarial talents. She regularly came up with good ideas for features, and once or twice lately, Loveday had suggested that she join her when she interviewed people. Keri was more than just a member of her editorial team: she and her artist boyfriend, Ben Poldavy, had become good friends of Loveday's.

Loveday tried not to think about the

day's events as she drove to their tiny, ramshackle cottage outside St Ives. It was at the end of a long, rutted lane, and on a starless night such as this, the place was in total blackness.

Keri must have been watching for her, because before Loveday had stopped and turned off the engine, she had flung open the door, flooding the lane with light.

'Hurry up, Loveday,' she called, doing a little dance on her doorstep. 'It's freezing out here.'

As she went in, Ben called a greeting from the kitchen, where he was stirring something on the stove. Appetizing meaty smells were filling the cottage. Loveday handed over the bottle of wine she'd brought and followed Keri through to the bright front room, where the well-scratched and -scrubbed wooden table had been set with three places. She sniffed the air.

'What are we having?'

'It's only spag bol, I'm afraid,' Keri said.

'Less of the 'only',' Ben called indignantly. 'There's nothing ordinary about my spag bol.'

They all laughed, and Keri poured three glasses of red wine.

Ben had been right. His supper was delicious. When she'd cleaned her plate, Loveday sank back in her chair, feeling pleasantly full and contented.

'So, Sam's busy tonight? What's he doing?' Keri asked.

Loveday took a breath.

'Working . . . he's working.'

She saw Keri and Ben exchange a look. She sighed.

'I wasn't going to tell you this . . . well, not yet. We think there may have been a murder in Marazion.'

They both stared at her wide-eyed, so Loveday recounted the day's events, leaving out the bit about her and Sam splitting up the previous night.

'God, that's awful,' Ben said. 'Do they know who did it?'

'Actually, the police are not a hundred per cent certain it *was* murder, but it's more than likely.' She'd said too much already. She hadn't planned on bringing this up tonight. 'Look you two, it's been a really stressful day. Do you mind if we don't . . . ?'

'You don't want to talk about it, of course you don't,' Keri said quickly. 'We completely understand.'

She looked at Ben. 'But actually, Loveday, there was something I wanted to ask you about.' She glanced up and met her friend's eyes. 'Have you noticed the strange mood that Merrick has been in lately? I'm beginning to get quite worried about him.'

Magazine owner, Merrick Tremayne, was regarded by his staff as more of a kindly father figure than a boss. The Tremaynes were a well-respected Truro family, even though their wealth had diminished over the years, mainly due to the magazine's catastrophic loss of circulation. The sensible thing would have been to sell it and cut their losses, accepting that they couldn't beat modern technology. But Merrick had refused to give in, even though it was a struggle to keep the organization running.

Since he'd taken Loveday on as assistant editor three years earlier, they had turned the ailing magazine around; and, although it was still run on a

46

shoestring, the circulation figures were beginning to climb.

Loveday had turned down more than one attempt to headhunt her over the last year, remaining staunchly loyal to Merrick. Although the fact that he was also Sam's best friend might also have influenced her.

But, now that Keri had mentioned it, Loveday had noticed that Merrick wasn't quite himself lately. He was distracted, and recently she'd seen him being short-tempered with staff, which wasn't at all like him. But she'd had her own problems to deal with, and had let it pass.

Keri was looking worried.

'You don't think he's ill, do you?'

Ben reached across and squeezed Keri's hand.

'You care too much about people . . . that's your problem, chicken.'

She gave him a weak smile and then turned back to Loveday.

'You're close to him, Loveday.' She paused. 'Maybe you could talk to him.'

Keri's words ran through her head as she drove home. It was true. Merrick was a friend. She just wasn't sure he would appreciate her interference in this. The word immediately reminded her of Sam. Wasn't this exactly what he was forever accusing her of?

Sam! Of course. She slapped the steering wheel. He should be the one to speak to Merrick. And at the very next opportunity, she would ask him.

4

Loveday was up early next morning. Over her first cup of coffee she had decided against her usual jog along the seafront. An interview on her digital recorder had to be transcribed, and that meant a trip to the office.

Lemon Street, where the magazine had its editorial offices, was mostly given over to professional premises these days. In the past, the elegant thoroughfare would have been where the city's wealthy businessmen had their homes. Several high-class restaurants had set up in recent years, but at this hour they were not yet open for business, so the normally busy street was quiet.

No one was working at the *Cornish Folk* offices that morning, and the premises were locked up. The only other person who had a key, apart from her and Merrick, was the lady in charge of the cleaning team — and they wouldn't be here on a Sunday.

It felt odd driving into the deserted office car park. Loveday pulled into her space and cut the engine. She got out and crossed to the staff entrance and let herself into the building, being careful to lock the door behind her again. Then she ran up the stairs to the first-floor office that Merrick called his 'editorial suite'. It was just a large, open-plan room with six desks. Merrick's own area was separated from the rest of the editorial floor by a glass partition.

Loveday sat down at her desk and powered up her computer before reaching into the drawer for her recorder and connecting up her earpiece. She typed solidly for an hour, only sitting up to stretch and massage the back of her neck when she had committed the entire interview to the screen.

Scanning through the text, she was pleased with the result. The subject of the interview, Sabine De Fries, had opened a boutique in Falmouth, specializing in lingerie and swimwear. It was Cassie who had suggested the glamorous young designer as a possible subject for a magazine article.

'If she's good enough for some of my snooty clients, then the girl's got talent,' she'd told Loveday over lunch in their favourite Truro bistro.

'Your clients have more money than sense, Cassie,' Loveday had teased. But she really admired her friend's savvy entrepreneurial instincts, and how she had set up her marine interior design business all on her own. Cassie provided upmarket makeovers for the insides of some of the most desirable luxury yachts in Cornwall's marinas.

Loveday was already imagining the picture spread they could get from the Sabine article. She was about to close down her computer when she heard the creak. Someone was moving about on the floor above.

She listened, her eyes on the ceiling. There it was again. There was definitely someone up there. Even if the cleaners had taken it upon themselves to come in on a Sunday, it wouldn't be one of them up on that floor, for it was just old files and unwanted office junk that had been stored there.

It could just be the settling of an old building. Loveday had heard somewhere that old buildings did that. Perhaps the office creaked all the time and no one noticed because the place was always so busy?

But the noise seemed to be moving around. It had to be an intruder. Loveday's heart was beginning to pound. She wondered what she should do. Calling the police was the obvious thing — but what if it was just a cat, or some other animal that had somehow got into the building and was now trapped up there? She would feel pretty stupid if she wasted police time on something like that. And what if Sam found out? How silly would that make her look?

She got up, moving cautiously to the door, and then to the foot of the stairs. She tried to swallow, but her mouth had gone dry. The dark, wooden stairs were uncarpeted and smelled musty. Slowly, she began to climb. Had the intruder come up these same stairs? But no, she reasoned, he wouldn't have a key, and there had been no sign of a break-in downstairs.

It crossed her mind that he could have come over the roofs of the neighbouring buildings and found an unsecured skylight window. But why risk such a dangerous climb? Apart from the computers, there was nothing of great value in the building, and certainly not up here in this part.

An icy shiver shot up her spine. What on earth was she doing? The sensible thing would be to get out of there fast. She could picture Sam's face when he heard about this. He wouldn't be pleased, but she couldn't turn back now.

Her trainers made no sound as she crept on. She'd only ever been up here a couple of times before, and was praying that none of the steps creaked.

Then she froze. She was almost certain she heard a door closing on one of the lower floors. She held her breath . . . listening again. But she was already so jumpy she could be imagining anything.

When she reached the door of the room where she thought the noise had come from, she paused. Her whole body tensed.

She listened. There was a grating noise, like the sound of drawers in an old metal filing cabinet being pulled open, and then slammed closed again. Paper was being rustled. Her heart was hammering so furiously now that she thought it might burst out of her chest.

She took a couple of slow deep breaths, trying to steady herself. She should have brought some kind of weapon with her. Loveday had no intention of tackling this intruder single-handed, but if he realized she was here, and suddenly charged out at her, she had no way of defending herself.

She stood for a moment, unsure of what to do next. Dared she open the door? She would have to if she wanted to know what was going on in there. She took another deep breath and slowly, inch by inch, eased the door open a fraction. She waited, expecting the intruder to rush at her at any moment, but the paper-rustling continued. There was faint nausea in the pit of her stomach. She took a quick gulp of air, and put her eye to the gap in the door.

She could see a man at the far side of

the room. She tried swallowing, but her throat had gone dry again. He had his back to her, but she could still tell he seemed too well-dressed for a regular burglar. So who was he? And what was he doing here in the magazine's offices?

She watched, fascinated, as he methodically went through drawer after drawer, extracting files and examining each one in turn. What was he after? She couldn't chance waiting to find out. She was about to move away when the man turned, his eyes scanning the room as though he was trying to remember where he'd left something.

Loveday ducked out of sight, her heart pounding even faster. He hadn't spotted her, but she had recognized him. She'd only seen him once before, but she was sure. He was Cadan Tremayne, Merrick's brother. She held her breath, her back pressed hard against the wall as she tried to make sense of this. She'd heard the stories of how Cadan had fought Merrick for control of the company . . . and of how he'd lost!

Slowly, she backed away, and slipped

back down the stairs as quietly as she could manage. This was none of her business. She was still shaking when she reached the car park. With trembling hands she switched on the Clio's ignition and cruised quietly out into Lemon Street.

The shops didn't open until lunchtime on Sundays, so for the moment the city streets were deserted. Well, not completely, for Loveday had caught a sudden movement to her left, as someone stepped quickly into a doorway when she drove past. The movement had seemed so furtive that she glanced back, but there was no one in sight. Frowning, she turned back to the road and drove out of the city.

All the way home she went over all the possibilities of why Cadan Tremayne would be rooting about in the magazine's old files. It made no sense. What could he possibly have been looking for? There had definitely been no sign of a break-in, so he must have had a key. Had he taken Merrick's key without his knowledge? Could whatever Cadan had been searching for be the reason for her boss's recent mood changes?

Loveday arrived back in Marazion to find Sam on her doorstep. He raised his hands in a gesture of defence when he saw her expression.

'It's not a social call,' he said quickly.

'Right,' Loveday said curtly. 'Well, in that case, you'd better come in.'

He walked beside her round to the back door and followed her into the kitchen.

'Sit down, Sam.' She indicated a kitchen chair, unable to keep the frosty glint from her eye. 'Or would you rather conduct your interview in the comfort of my sitting-room?'

Sam's brow came down and he scowled at her.

'Why are you being so teasy? You knew I would have to speak to you again.'

Loveday couldn't help smiling at his use of the old Cornish word for 'bad-tempered', but he was right. She was being deliberately awkward, and she didn't know why, especially since she wanted his help over Merrick.

'Okay,' she said, dragging out a chair and sitting down on it.

Sam was still standing. He glanced to the clock on the wall. It was a relic from her parents' pub, and bore a picture of a grouse, advertising a famous Scottish whisky.

'Have you eaten yet?' he asked.

She looked up, trying to hide her surprise. Was he inviting her to lunch?

'I thought you were on duty.'

'Even policemen have to eat,' he said.

Loveday shrugged.

'Fine.'

She picked up the leather jacket she had only just discarded, and slipped it back on.

They left the cottage and began walking up the drive. As they passed the big house where Cassie and her family lived, Loveday saw the front room curtains twitch and knew Cassie had spotted them. She couldn't see her face, but she knew she would be smiling. She obviously didn't know Sam's visit was not a social call. He had made that very clear.

They walked along the front in silence, both knowing without either of them saying that they were headed for the

Godolphin Hotel, where the dining-room windows looked out over Mounts Bay. It was one of their favourite eating places, but Loveday was taking no comfort from that today. It also happened to be convenient if you didn't want to leave Marazion.

The waiter recognized them and came forward, smiling.

'Your usual table's free if you've come for lunch.'

They followed him to the table with the best view of St Michael's Mount and the causeway, at which they had previously shared so many romantic dinners.

Loveday sat down, forcing her mind to stay focused on the present. This was a Sunday lunch, not some amorous encounter. And she was being interviewed by a police officer in connection with a possible murder enquiry.

The waiter brought their menus, and pointed out that the carvery was open. They both decided on that and picked their way through the tables to collect a plate and make their choices.

Sam hadn't ordered his usual bottle of

wine, but simply asked Loveday what she wanted to drink. They both had half-pints of lager.

Despite having eaten her fill at Keri and Ben's place the previous evening, Loveday realized that she was once again ravenous. She didn't normally eat this much. Stress must have given her an appetite.

The meal seemed to have mellowed Sam, for when the waiter returned to remove their empty plates, he was grinning at her.

'I've never seen you eat like that before, Loveday. Have you been starving yourself?'

She wished he would stop using her name in that teasing, intimate way. Had he forgotten they had split up? She cleared her throat.

'You said something about needing to speak to me about Jago Tilley.'

Sam frowned.

'I don't think I said that; but now that you've brought up the subject, perhaps you could tell me how you knew him?'

Loveday looked up, surprised.

'But I didn't. I've never met the man.'

It was Sam's turn for surprise.

'Sorry . . . from the way Mrs Rodda spoke about you and Cassie, I assumed that you both kept a kindly eye on him.'

Loveday shrugged.

'The only thing I know about the man is what Priddy told me yesterday.'

'Which was . . . ?'

'That he was a regular at the Five Stars, and had been drinking there last night, and that he has a relative who is a bad lot.' She glanced up, saw Sam was studying her, and was annoyed to find herself blushing. 'She said this nephew, Billy Travis, had a police record, and that you would know all about him.'

Sam nodded.

'That's more or less what she told us last night.' He looked at his watch. 'We brought him in for questioning this morning. He's waiting to be interviewed right now.'

Loveday glanced across to the Mount. The December days were short, and lights had already begun to glow in some of the castle windows. She could see a Christmas tree twinkling on the harbour quay.

'Why would anyone want to kill a nice old chap like that, Sam?' She spoke softly, still touched by Priddy's obvious devotion to her friend.

'We don't know for sure that anyone did kill him . . . at least, not yet. We won't have the post-mortem results until the morning.' He sighed. 'But anything other than foul play is unlikely.' He spread his fingers out on the table and stared at them. 'And to answer your question . . . I just haven't a clue. Jago Tilley doesn't appear to have been a wealthy man.'

'He only had his cottage,' Loveday cut in, 'and that's going to a fishermen's charity in Newlyn.'

Sam stared at her.

'The Newlyn Fishermen's Federation? Who told you that?'

'Priddy did. She said she went with Jago to his solicitor's office in Penzance to witness his will. Billy inherits nothing.' A sudden thought struck her. 'Do you think he found out and was trying to persuade Jago to change his will?'

Sam suddenly got to his feet, reaching into his pocket for his mobile phone.

'Excuse me for a minute, Loveday.'

He disappeared into the hotel foyer, leaving her staring after him.

She knew at once what he was doing. If Billy Travis knew the old man had cut him out of his will, it could give him a reason for attacking his uncle . . . and one of Sam's team was about to interview him. He would be telling them to hold off until he arrived back at the station himself.

Sam came back to the table and sat down, his expression thoughtful.

'So what else did Priddy tell you?'

Loveday shrugged.

'That was about it.' She was trying to work out if he was annoyed with her for knowing something that he hadn't. It was hardly her fault if people confided in her. His next question surprised her.

'What did you see when you went into Jago's house?'

She frowned.

'How do you mean?'

'Try to take yourself back to that instant when you looked into the cottage.'

Loveday narrowed her eyes, trying to

snap her mind back to the moment.

'I didn't exactly go into the cottage. Adam told Priddy and I to stay at the door.' She hesitated. 'I saw the body, of course . . . and the blood. I could see Adam's attention had been drawn up to the landing at the top of the stairs. The carpet was ruffled, and there were marks on the wall.'

'Marks?'

'You know . . . scratching, streaks of blood.' She glanced across at him. 'But you saw all this for yourself.'

Sam nodded.

'Anything else? Think, Loveday. Try to visualize exactly what was there.'

Loveday shut her eyes. The hall had been gloomy, dark varnish everywhere. There had been a kitchen down at the far end. It was just an ordinary cottage.

She squeezed her eyes tighter shut . . . concentrating. The door into the room on her right had been partially open and she had glimpsed the interior of a sitting-room. There had been a big, grey upholstered armchair and some faded pictures on the wall.

Her eyes flew open.

'A picture was missing.'

Sam's head jerked up.

'There was a patch of wallpaper above and to the right of the fireplace that was a few shades lighter than the rest.'

She sat up, giving him a triumphant smile.

'Someone had removed a picture. Is that what you wanted me to remember?'

His expression gave nothing away.

'You've done well, Loveday. Thank you.'

Her journalist's mind was whirring. She had a shedload of questions, all of which she knew he would not answer. She would have to work out the significance of the missing picture for herself. Priddy would know what used to hang there — and she was pretty sure that Sam would have already asked her. So what had that piece of theatre been about? Was he setting her a riddle? Was he asking for her help without using the words?

If she asked him outright he would warn her off, and they would have another row. She didn't want that. She hadn't yet asked him about Merrick.

She suddenly decided the best way to approach that was head-on.

'I'm worried about Merrick,' she said.

Sam put his empty glass on the table and gave her a quizzical frown.

'You haven't noticed?'

His shoulders lifted in a shrug.

'I haven't seen Merrick in over a week.'

'Isn't that in itself a bit odd? I thought you two were joined at the hip.'

'Well, hardly,' he grimaced. 'But you're right. I should ring him.'

Loveday bit her lip, wondering how much she should tell him. She decided just to wade in.

'There's something else.'

Sam looked at her from under his brow.

'I was in the office this morning, and . . . well, I thought I heard someone moving about upstairs. It was odd because there were no cars in the car park, and I'd thought the building was empty.' She swallowed. 'So I went to check.'

Sam rolled his eyes to the ceiling.

'Loveday!' His voice was incredulous.

'I *was* going to call the police,' she protested. 'I just wanted to make sure I wouldn't be wasting their time.'

She glanced quickly around the nearby tables to make sure there was no one in earshot.

'It was Cadan,' she whispered.

Sam's eyebrows shot up.

'Merrick's brother?'

Loveday nodded.

'He was definitely up to something, Sam. I saw him rifling through the files in the old storage cabinets.'

'Why would he do that?'

She shrugged.

'I have no idea, but he must have had a key to the building. None of the doors had been forced.'

'Maybe Merrick asked him to look for something,' he suggested.

But she could tell by his expression that he didn't believe that any more than she did. She waited for a moment before speaking.

'Do you think we should tell Merrick?'

Sam pouted, considering this.

'Let me think about it,' he said, checking his watch. 'But right now I have to get back to the station.'

5

Sam lost no time driving back to Truro. This was one interview he had to handle himself. It wasn't yet four o'clock, but it was almost dark as he pulled into the police car park.

He felt a buzz of excitement as he ran up the stairs to the CID suite. Will Tregellis had a phone clamped to his ear and looked up as Sam strode past, beckoning him into his small office.

'I take it this is about Travis, boss,' he said, ending his call and hurrying after Sam.

Sam nodded. 'I want you with me when I interview him.'

Travis was drumming his fingers on the table as the detectives walked in, and he fixed Sam with a venomous glare.

'I've been here two sodding hours, and I've done nothing bloody wrong.' The man made to get up. 'I've had enough. I'm getting out of here right now.'

Sam put a hand on Travis's shoulder. 'Sit down, Billy. No one's been keeping you here against your will. You haven't been arrested. You're here to help with our enquiries.'

Billy threw himself back onto his chair. 'Ten minutes . . . that's all you're getting, and then I'm out of here.'

Sam sat down and opened the file he had brought with him, examining the contents before looking up. He said, 'Your uncle Jago has just died in suspicious circumstances. Don't you want to help us find his killer?'

A nervous tic had begun to twitch at the corner of the man's mouth.

'Well, I had nothing to do with it. Why are you questioning me?'

The defiance in his voice didn't match the body language. Billy Travis was nervous — or was it guilt? Sam wasn't yet sure.

The man folded his arms. 'Okay, is this where I get the third degree?'

Sam gave him a hard stare, holding it until Travis unfolded his arms again and began to squirm in his seat.

'You don't look too upset by your uncle's death, Billy.'

Billy glanced away, and Sam saw the tic at his mouth start twitching again. 'We didn't get on, me and him.' He looked down, fidgeting with his hands.

Sam and Will waited.

Billy shrugged. 'He might have been my uncle, but he was a nasty old bugger, and mean as they come. Ask anybody.'

'In what way was he mean, Billy?' Sam said. 'Are you saying he was cruel . . . threatening . . . what?'

'I'm saying he was family, and he treated me like rubbish. Even when I was down on my luck he refused to help. God knows what happened to the money he got for his boat, but none of it came my way.'

'You sound quite bitter about that, Billy,' Will said, responding to Sam's nod. They watched the man shrug. 'Was that it, Billy? Were you bitter? Bitter enough to kill the old man?'

'What?' Billy sprang forward, eyes blazing. But Sam waved him back down.

'We're just trying to get to the truth,

70

Billy. Just answer the sergeant's questions and we'll all get along fine.'

'Is that why I'm here? You think I murdered the old codger?' His eyes were wide with fear now. 'I didn't kill him. Why would I kill him?'

Sam picked up his pen, casually rolling it between his fingers. 'Yes, why would you?' he said slowly. 'After all, who else would Mr Tilley leave his cottage to?'

'What?' Travis was wary. 'Why shouldn't the cottage come to me? I'm his only family.'

'Maybe you got fed up waiting for what you considered your inheritance, and bumped the old man off,' Will said, raising an eyebrow.

'That's rubbish. The old geezer was on his last legs anyway. I wouldn't have had long to wait.'

Sam studied the man's indignant face. He was inclined to believe him. Billy Travis knew nothing about his uncle's will. But neither was he completely innocent.

'Where were you at ten o'clock on Friday night, Billy?' Sam asked.

Billy ran a hand over his shaved head

and his brows came down. 'I had a skinful on Friday. I don't bloody know where I was.'

'So you don't have an alibi for the time of your uncle's death?' Sam said evenly.

'What? Of course I have a bloody alibi. I wasn't bloody there, was I?'

'So where were you then, Billy?' he said.

'I can't tell you what I don't know, but I didn't bloody kill him.'

All trace of pretence had now completely slipped away.

Billy's eyes rolled to the ceiling and his brow furrowed as he desperately searched for an answer.

Then he snapped his fingers and grinned. 'The Hog's Head in Penzance . . . that's where I was.' He sat back and blew out his cheeks. 'I was in the bloody Hog's Head. They had a lock-in. I remember now. I didn't get back to my caravan until the early hours.'

Sam nodded to Will, and both men stood up.

'You won't mind enjoying our hospitality for a little longer, Billy while we check out your story.'

'But I've told you where I was,' Billy insisted. 'I couldn't have been in Penzance and Marazion at the same time, now could I?'

'We'll follow it up, and if what you've told us checks out then you'll be off the hook.' Sam smiled as he and Will left the room.

'An hour, that's all you're having,' Travis shouted after them. 'And I'll be wanting my bloody supper while I'm waiting.'

It was more than an hour before they got the confirmation that the man's alibi stood up. The landlord of the Hog's Head had at first been reluctant to confirm Billy's story of after-hours drinking that Friday night; but when DC Amanda Fox had pointed out the seriousness of a suspicious death inquiry, he relented and admitted that Billy had been in the pub at the significant time.

'I think he was telling the truth, sir,' she told Sam over the phone. 'Billy Travis would seem to be in the clear.'

* * *

Loveday had known she would get a visit from Cassie as soon as Sam had driven away, but it was a while after he left before she heard the tap on the back door.

'You're slipping,' Loveday teased, checking her watch. 'I was expecting you hours ago.'

Cassie made a face.

'Am I that obvious?'

'Uh-huh.'

Loveday opened the fridge and took out a bottle of white wine.

'Now that you're here, I suppose I'll have to ply you with strong drink.'

Cassie gave her one of her innocent stares.

'Now, what other reason would I have for calling to see an old grump like you?'

Loveday shook her head, laughing, as she took a couple of glasses from the cupboard.

'Let's take this through to the fire.'

'I saw Sam leaving earlier,' Cassie said, giving Loveday one of her mischievous looks. 'Does that mean you two are back together again?'

'Not at all. He wanted to talk about Jago Tilley.'

'Oh,' Cassie said, disappointed. She wanted to probe further, but could tell from her friend's expression that her relationship with Sam was not up for discussion.

'What did he want to know about Jago?'

Loveday filled two glasses and handed one to Cassie. She took a sip of her cold wine and stared into the fire.

'He thought I knew him . . . from before, I mean; but I've never even met the man.'

'I knew him,' Cassie said. 'He's been out in the dinghy with Adam a couple of times. He used to be a fisherman until he sold his boat.' She screwed up her face, trying to remember the name of the boat, and smiled when it came back to her. 'The *Maria* . . . that was it. He sold it to someone up Padstow way, but I think he always regretted that. He was lost without that old boat.'

'Then why get rid of it?'

Cassie shrugged.

'I suppose he needed the money . . . or maybe it just got too much for him to handle. From what I've heard, he seemed to spend most of his time in the pub latterly.' She pouted. 'He was a wily old devil. There was always some tourist or other gullible enough to listen to his old seafaring stories in exchange for a pint.' She blinked. 'Or was that the other one?'

'Other one?' Loveday queried.

Cassie nodded. 'Yes, he hung around with old Harry Tasker. They were always together. Quite a double act as I remember.' She shook her head, and added thoughtfully, 'Poor Harry. He's going to miss his old pal.'

Loveday smiled. She was sorry she hadn't actually met the old man. Then a thought struck her.

'Have you ever been inside Jago's cottage, Cassie?'

'No, and I don't think many other people have, apart from Priddy.'

The conversation turned to work, and Loveday thanked her friend again for suggesting she should interview the Falmouth boutique owner, Sabine De Fries.

Her mind scrolled back to her meeting

with the elegant, blonde Dutch woman. Sabine had suggested turning up for the interview on a Monday, which she had explained was usually a quiet day. It meant she could close the shop for a lunch break.

She remembered the woman's attractive accent and her stylish clothes. But there had been a glint of steel in the provocative emerald eyes that suggested Sabine De Fries would take no prisoners as she climbed the ladder of success. And that was definitely where she was going.

Loveday had been impressed when she entered the Falmouth boutique and the glamorous vision that was Sabine came smiling towards her.

Her simple black silk blouse and pencil skirt that stopped just above the knee could have been dowdy on someone else, but Sabine had knotted a filmy scarlet scarf at her throat. Loveday was reminded of a beautiful exotic butterfly. Glancing down at her own smart navy M&S two-piece, she resisted the urge to frown.

She followed the woman into a spacious back room that was lined with open metal shelves stacked with boxes of stock. A collection of empty picture frames lay against the wall. Loveday's gaze went to the window at the far end, where she knew there would be a spectacular view of Falmouth Harbour. Most of the shops on this side of the road enjoyed that wonderful vista from the back windows of their properties. Sabine was obviously security-conscious, for there was a strong wire grille covering the glass.

She led the way past a tiny kitchen and staff washroom, and then up a flight of stairs to the living accommodation.

Loveday stifled a gasp as she emerged into a stunning open-plan room. Sliding glass doors at the far end led onto a small balcony that overlooked the harbour. Apart from the dark oak floor that ran throughout, the only colours in the glamorous apartment were silver and white.

Sabine smiled.

'You like it?'

Loveday thought of her own homely little cottage, with its higgledy-piggledy arrangement of bookcases, the unsteady table that housed her laptop, and the overcrowded wardrobe, and sighed.

'It's lovely,' she murmured. And it was. It just wasn't a place where she could comfortably live. She glanced through the open bedroom door where, apart from a dark, expensive-looking oil painting hanging over the huge bed, the white and silver theme continued.

'The bathroom's just through there if you'd like to freshen up before we eat,' Sabine said, nodding towards the back of the room.

'Thanks.' Loveday smiled. 'I'll only be a minute and then I'll give you a hand in the kitchen.'

'No need,' Sabine called after her. 'It's nothing elaborate.'

The bathroom was surprisingly large for such a compact flat, and here the colour scheme was a pale grey. A roll-top bath stood on marble tiles, and the shower looked a lot more luxurious than the cramped affair Loveday had at the cottage.

It took a few moments to work out how to turn on the gleaming chrome taps. As she dried her hands on a thick white towel, her eye was drawn to a shelf of expensive toiletries along the side of the bath. There was a bottle of men's after-shave. On closer inspection, Loveday could see a tub of gent's moisturizing lotion. She thought about having a sneaky look inside the corner cabinet for more evidence of a man friend, but that would have been too much like spying on her hostess. Sabine's love life was none of her business.

Sabine had set the small glass table by the balcony window for lunch. Loveday murmured her approval as plates of chicken salad and a basket of crusty bread were produced.

'This looks delicious, but you really shouldn't have gone to all this trouble, Sabine.'

The woman waved her words aside.

'First we eat, and then we talk,' she said.

It wasn't the way Loveday usually conducted her interviews, but if that was the way Sabine wanted it, then she would get no complaints from her.

After the meal Loveday reached into her bag for her notebook, also bringing out her digital recorder.

Sabine's eyebrow went up a fraction.

'I won't use the recorder if you're not comfortable about it,' Loveday said. 'It just helps with my notes, and everything gets erased at the end of the day.'

The woman raised her long slim fingers. 'It's fine. I don't mind it.'

For the next hour Loveday listened to Sabine describing her early days in Amsterdam, from where her parents, Erik and Frieda De Fries, still ran their small empire of boutique hotels. She described her time at a Swiss finishing school, and then at a Paris art college, where she honed her design skills.

It was all a long way from the little Falmouth boutique. Loveday was curious. What was the woman doing here? Whatever the reason, her story would make a great magazine feature.

She smiled, settling back into the interview.

'So, Sabine. What actually brought you to Cornwall?'

Sabine turned her wide green eyes on Loveday and smiled.

'It's so beautiful here, don't you think?'

'Well, yes. But Paris and Amsterdam are also beautiful.' She shrugged. 'Even London has its attractions.'

'Ah, but it doesn't have the ambiance . . . the big skies . . . the incredible light.'

Loveday stopped writing and looked up. It was an artist's description of Cornwall. She remembered the picture frames she'd spotted in Sabine's storeroom.

'Do you paint, Sabine?' she asked, suddenly curious.

The woman smiled, but not before Loveday had noticed the brief spark of irritation that had flickered in the green eyes.

'All design is art . . . don't you think?'

The street was busier when Loveday emerged from the boutique, having arranged a time for her photographer, Mylor Ennis, to go along for his photoshoot.

As she walked slowly back to her car she was aware that she was still none the wiser as to why Sabine De Fries had set up her business in a Cornish seaside resort when she could have chosen any of Europe's great fashion cities.

Cassie's voice brought her back to the present.

'I'm glad that worked out,' she was saying. 'Sabine's a bit of a mystery, but I would never have put her down as a doormat.'

'You'll have to explain that,' Loveday said, setting her glass down on the low coffee table between them, and fixing her friend with a questioning stare.

Cassie tucked her legs under her and took another sip of wine before going on. 'Well, she's the last person I would have suspected of putting her business at risk for a man, but the word is that she's been dipping into her profits to fund this bloke's gambling debts.'

Loveday thought of the icily cool businesswoman she had interviewed. She'd never met anyone quite so supremely confident. Loveday couldn't imagine any man cracking that professional veneer. She sat forward.

'So who is this man?'

'Ah, well; the grapevine hasn't got that far yet, but as soon as I know, then . . . '

'No,' Loveday laughed, putting her hand up. 'Don't bother. I'm not that desperate. But I do appreciate you coming over tonight, Cassie. It hasn't been an easy day.'

She hadn't intended telling her friend about the Cadan incident, but she did.

Cassie's eyes widened.

'What could he have been looking for?'

Loveday shrugged, getting up to refill their glasses. But Cassie put her hand over hers.

'No, not for me, thanks. I only popped out for a few minutes. Adam will think I've moved in here.'

Loveday poured a few inches of wine into her own glass and went back to her chair.

'I don't know what he was looking for, but he was searching for something — and I got the distinct impression that Merrick knew nothing about it. They might be brothers, but there's no love lost between them.'

Cassie got to her feet.

'I really must go, but I'll want to hear the follow-up to this Cadan story.'

'Me too,' Loveday said, following her friend to the door.

★　★　★

The next morning wasn't one for jogging on the beach. It had snowed again during the night, and although it had stopped now, a heavy grey pall hung over Mounts Bay. Cocooned in her duvet, Loveday felt too comfortable to get up, so she treated herself to another ten minutes as she thought about the day ahead.

She had made appointments to interview two people for future articles; not too onerous a task, she thought. It should be a fairly easy day.

Her mind drifted to Sam, and she wondered if he was planning to meet up with Merrick later. Maybe they would invite her to join them at the pub? But, no — she screwed up her face — that would defeat the purpose of the man-to-man chat she assumed Sam was planning.

Reluctantly, she climbed out of bed,

pulled on her robe, and went into the kitchen to make toast and a pot of strong coffee. Fifteen minutes later, showered and dressed, she stood at her bedroom window. The snow had muffled all the usual early-morning sounds, making the outside world seem eerily quiet.

By the time she set off for the city, the picture had changed. The snowploughs had been out, and the main roads were mainly clear. It still didn't help with the usual slow crawl to work; which, to Loveday's irritation, seemed to take longer than ever this morning.

Keri glanced up from her computer screen as Loveday walked into the office.

'Well?' She raised an expectant eyebrow. 'Any more about what we should do about Merrick?'

Loveday glanced across to Merrick's office, where she could see he appeared to be having a disagreement with someone on the phone.

'I've spoken to Sam about it,' she said. 'He's going to have a word with him.'

'Let's hope it's a good word, then. I'm fed up getting my head bitten off every time I speak to him.'

Loveday slanted another look back to her boss, and frowned. It wasn't like Merrick to snap people's heads off, whether he had reason to or not.

'That chap who does the beach sculptures is coming in this morning,' Keri reminded her, as she scanned through the diary.

But Loveday's mind was already on something else . . . it was a crazy idea, but she felt she had to do more than just rely on Sam speaking to Merrick.

'I might have to go out for a while this morning, Keri. How do you feel about interviewing our sculpture artist?'

Her friend's face lit up.

'You mean it?'

Loveday grinned at her.

'I don't see why not. You're more than capable.'

Loveday was still smiling as she slipped her red wool coat back on and headed out of the office.

Morvah, the Tremayne family home, was a large converted farmhouse just a few miles out of Truro. Loveday had the notion of just turning up at the door, but she could hardly do that when Merrick wasn't at home.

The only other people who lived there were his elderly father, Edward Tremayne, and the pair's attractive, middle-aged housekeeper, Connie Bishop.

The low white bar gates stood invitingly open, giving a clear view up the curving drive to the house. Loveday cruised slowly past, pulling up slightly beyond the gates, still with no real idea what to do next.

She should have thought this through. If she wasn't careful, she could make a monumental fool of herself — and how would she explain that to her boss? She sat for a few minutes, chewing her lip and glancing back at the house. There was no sign of life.

She sighed. If she drove off now without even trying to do something, she would be cross with herself all day. She took a deep breath, released the catch that opened the bonnet, and then got out, walking round the front of the car to prop the bonnet open. It was a weak ploy, but if she went up to the house and explained that she'd come out without her phone and asked to use theirs, she was unlikely to be refused.

She started walking towards the gates when a small white sports car shot past her and turned up to the house. The wheels screeched as the driver made an emergency stop, scattering gravel in all directions. He got out and began striding back towards her.

'Got a problem?' Cadan Tremayne's flint-blue eyes narrowed as he studied her in a way that made Loveday feel uncomfortable. Her gaze swept over the faded blue jeans, the casual dark-green silk shirt under the tan-coloured suede jacket. The distinctive tan-and-white leather shoes looked Italian. She swallowed.

An image of Cadan, rummaging through those files in Merrick's office, flashed through her mind. She concentrated on staying calm. There was no way he could know that she'd seen him.

However, they had met once before, although he didn't seem to recognize her now. It had been three years back, when she'd arrived at the magazine office to be interviewed by Merrick for the job of assistant editor. She and Cadan had met on the stairs. He'd played a silly game, refusing to let her pass until she agreed to have a drink with him. Loveday had not been amused. The man was too arrogant for words, and she certainly had no intention of wasting any more time on him than she had already been forced to.

At the sound of approaching footsteps, Cadan had turned, and Loveday took her chance to push past him and hurry on up the stairs.

The interview with Merrick Tremayne had gone even better than she'd hoped and she'd joined the staff the very next week as assistant editor.

Merrick had since taken a step back from the day-to-day running of things, putting Loveday in sole charge of the editorial. It was only later she found out the young man who had accosted her on the stairs had been Merrick's brother.

She hadn't liked Cadan Tremayne back then, and from what she could see now, he hadn't changed any. He was still appraising her with an impudent grin.

Loveday nodded back to her car.

'It just stopped,' she said helplessly, glancing up at the house. 'I know the people here so I was hoping to use their phone. I seem to have left mine in the office.'

Cadan's eyes became slits.

'And you would be?'

Loveday stuck out her hand.

'Loveday Ross. My boss lives here.' She paused, squinting up at him, repeating his own question. 'And you would be?'

Cadan took her hand and introduced himself.

'I'll have a look at your car.' He turned and began walking towards the Clio.

'Oh, there's really no need,' Loveday protested. 'It's such a temperamental old thing. It keeps letting me down.' Her mind was reeling, trying to work out how she could explain that there was absolutely nothing wrong with it.

'You get in and start the engine,' he instructed. 'I'll see if I can spot the problem.'

Cadan's blond head disappeared under the bonnet. She switched on the engine, and it purred into life.

'Sounds all right now,' he said, still

peering at the works. 'You probably just flooded it. I should take it to a garage and have it checked over anyway.'

If he was suspicious he wasn't showing it.

'But now that you're here . . . ' He gave her another teasing grin. ' . . . and since you're practically a member of the family . . . why don't you come in and join us for lunch? I'm sure my father would appreciate the company.'

Loveday's cheeks were burning. Her mind was tracking through all the reasons she could give for refusing. What could she possibly learn about Merrick's problems by having lunch with his father and brother? It wasn't as if she could actually *ask* them what was worrying her boss. On the other hand, she was here now . . .

Cadan was leading her back to his car. He opened the passenger door.

'Hop in. I'll take you up. We apparently eat in the kitchen here during the day. I take it that will be all right with you?'

He gunned the engine, and the little car shot forward the hundred yards up the drive, skidding to a halt at the front steps.

Cadan got out and led the way to the front door, which he threw open, calling for the housekeeper.

Connie Bishop arrived with a smart click of heels on the stone flagging of the hall floor.

'We have a visitor, Connie. Can you squeeze another one from the pot?'

The woman's face lit up in surprise when she recognized Loveday.

'Miss Ross! How nice to see you.' She stood back to let them pass her. 'Mr Tremayne is in his sitting-room, I'll just tell him you're here.'

Edward Tremayne was in a high-backed upholstered armchair, smoking his pipe and gazing at the leaping flames in the fireplace. He started to struggle to his feet when Loveday walked into the room, but she waved him back down. He looked frailer than the last time she'd seen him.

'You remember Miss Ross, sir,' Connie said. 'She's Mr Merrick's editor at the magazine.'

'Well, of course I do. I'm not completely senile, Mrs Bishop . . . well, not yet, anyway.'

93

He gave Loveday a craggy smile and indicated she should sit.

Cadan strolled into the room behind her, and she didn't miss the scowl the old man gave his son.

Loveday had never been in this room on any of her previous visits to Morvah. It was a homely sanctuary, with high ceilings and rose-coloured walls. Two huge sash windows looked out over a rolling landscape of fields and hedgerows, crisp under a layer of snow. A faded floral carpet covered the floor, and beside the fire sat a large wicker basket piled high with logs. An old-fashioned set of bellows was propped up next to it.

Loveday's attention was drawn to a painting of some lopsided cottages around a strange little harbour. She was smiling at the naïvety of the work, and wondering why it looked familiar.

'Ah, I can see you are another fan of the wonderful Alfred Wallis,' Edward Tremayne said.

Loveday spun round. 'Alfred Wallis?'

Edward nodded. 'The St Ives artist. I thought you'd recognized his work.'

Of course, it was coming back to her now. Her artist friend, Lawrence Kemp, had mentioned him. Wallis was a fisherman who had turned out scores of these quirky paintings in his time. His work was now highly respected, and very sought after. The Tate in St Ives exhibited a collection of his paintings.

Loveday smiled. 'I can see why you like this painting. It's fun.'

'Exactly.' Edward shook his head. 'I had two of them, until a few weeks ago. The burglar knew what he was after. The painting he stole was worth a small fortune.'

Loveday was shocked. Merrick hadn't mentioned his home had been burgled.

'But that's awful, Mr Tremayne. I'm so sorry.'

'Yes, it was horrible,' Edward Tremayne said, his eyes on the remaining painting. 'I particularly liked that one.'

Cadan gave an impatient tut. 'It was only a picture, Father. And you still have the other one.'

Loveday stared at him. How could he be so callous when it was obvious how upset his father was at the loss of something he loved? She was about to tell him so when Edward Tremayne said, 'Cadan's right. That's enough of my sorrows. What brings you to see us, Miss Ross?'

'Her car broke down . . . just outside the gate, would you believe?' Cadan cut in.

'Do you need a garage to tow it away, is that it?' Edward Tremayne looked concerned.

'Actually, I think your son has managed to fix it,' Loveday said, noticing again how the old man flinched at the mention of his son.

Cadan Tremayne might be confident that he could charm the ladies, but it was clear he had few fans in this house.

The large farmhouse kitchen table had been set for four. Loveday glanced round admiringly as she walked in. A big green Aga filled an alcove, and above it was an old wooden clock that wouldn't have looked out of place in a Victorian railway station.

'I hope you like lentil soup, Miss Ross,' Connie said, as she dished it out. 'We all need something warm and nourishing inside us at this time of year.'

'It looks delicious,' Loveday murmured. 'But you must call me Loveday.'

'Does that go for all of us?' Cadan said, giving her that appraising look again.

She nodded.

'Of course.'

How could this man, who made her skin crawl, be even remotely related to Merrick?

A satisfyingly filling steak-and-kidney pie, with accompanying vegetables, followed the soup, which turned out to be every bit as tasty as it looked. Even though she'd declined the apple pie and cream that came later, Loveday felt that she had eaten more food in the last couple of days than she had in the entire previous week.

'I'll walk with you to the car,' Cadan insisted, after Loveday had said her thanks and made to leave.

She was almost at the door when his mobile phone rang. He dived into his pocket, pulled it out and frowned at the screen.

'I've been expecting this call. Do you

mind if I take it?'

Loveday murmured that she didn't, grateful for the opportunity to slip away without him. She was halfway down the gravel drive when she realized Connie Bishop was puffing up behind her.

'Can I have a quick word, Miss Ross?' she asked breathlessly. But before Loveday could answer, she said, 'Did Merrick send you?'

'Well, no. What made you ask that?'

Connie's eyes darted back to the house.

'You're a smart young woman. Merrick is always singing your praises.' She hesitated. 'You know about Cadan, don't you?'

'I know Merrick isn't happy,' Loveday said. 'We've all been a bit worried about him back at the office.'

Connie Bishop bit her lip, her attention continuing to flick back to the house. 'I'm probably overstepping the mark telling you this, but I believe I can trust you, Miss . . . Loveday. Cadan's come back to cause trouble. I'm not exactly sure what he's up to, but . . . ' She left the sentence unfinished.

Loveday touched her arm.

'Connie, I saw him searching through the magazine's old files when he thought the office was empty on Sunday. Have you any idea what he could have been looking for?'

Connie shook her head.

'There's a man called Caine . . . Rupert Caine, who keeps calling, and he seems to put the fear of death into Cadan. Could it be anything to do with him?'

'Rupert Caine,' Loveday repeated. 'Do you know anything about him?'

'Only that he has some kind of vehicle company.' She gave Loveday a shy smile. 'I looked him up on the laptop.'

The man's name was familiar, Loveday reflected as she drove back to the office. But who was he?

As soon as she got back to her desk, she Googled the name 'Rupert Caine'. A list of different options, all containing the man's name, filled the screen. They appeared to be mostly newspaper articles about a company that bought and sold classic cars. According to what she was reading, 'Rupert Caine Classic Cars' seemed to be the main UK supplier of specialist vehicles to film and TV companies, not to mention wealthy collectors.

There were several pictures of the elderly, silver-haired Rupert. Loveday stared at the images trying to imagine why a telephone call from this man would strike the kind of fear into Cadan that Connie Bishop had suggested.

She could see him buying a car from the elegant Rupert — but even if he got into debt and couldn't afford to keep up payments, he would simply have to give the vehicle back.

Loveday sighed. She wasn't really any further forward in helping Merrick. She glanced over to his office and saw that he wasn't at his desk. It wasn't like him to take late lunches in the middle of the week. It crossed her mind that he might have gone home. If he had, would they tell him that she had been there earlier?

She knew she was meddling again in something that was really nothing to do with her; but she had a feeling that her boss was in trouble, and if she didn't do something to help him, then who would?

Turning her attention back to the computer screen, she clicked onto the next page, and frowned. There was a Rupe Caine who owned the Red Dragon Casino in Plymouth. She sat up. Now, this was much more Cadan's style. What if Merrick's half-brother was a gambler who had got himself into debt . . . serious debt?

6

Sam leaned back in his chair and frowned at the collection of witness statements spread on the desk. Billy Travis had been their main — their only — suspect so far, but his alibi had stood up. There was no evidence that he had been anywhere near Jago Tilley's cottage on the night the old man died. But he hadn't finished with that young rogue.

Statements from customers at the Five Stars Inn only confirmed their victim's drinking habits. By all accounts he had become a grouchy old devil in recent years, but then he was an elderly man, so maybe he was entitled. Apart from that, he apparently had no enemies. In fact, many of the locals said they liked Jago Tilley, even if that wasn't the picture his nephew had painted.

Murder still hadn't been confirmed, but there was no doubt in Sam's mind that it soon would be. So what had they had missed? He sighed and began to thumb his way through the statements again.

He had hoped the missing picture would produce something interesting, but according to Priddy, it had only been a sketched drawing of the victim's mother as a girl — precious to the old man, no doubt, but worthless to anyone else.

It still didn't explain what had happened to it. Had it fallen off the wall and smashed? Or had Jago removed it for some other reason? Priddy had been asked, but she could shed no light on the whereabouts of the picture.

It had been devious of him to involve Loveday in that, and he was regretting it now. He'd known she would make her own enquiries about the missing picture, so there was always the chance that she would stumble on something that had evaded him. She had a knack of winning people's confidence, and he was blatantly using her.

He pushed back his chair, stretched, and moved to the window, staring glumly down on the queuing traffic at the roundabout. The overnight snow had turned to slush, but the sky was still heavy and it looked like it was going to be one of those dank, overcast days that never really got light.

Sam glanced over the rooftops in the direction of Loveday's office. He could picture her busily tapping at her computer, chewing her bottom lip the way she did when she was concentrating, and he smiled.

She'd been worried about Merrick. Was she right, he wondered, to be so concerned? From what she'd told him, Merrick's brother Cadan had certainly been behaving oddly. What could he possibly have been searching for in cabinets of ancient and dusty files? He'd promised Loveday that he would speak to Merrick. Maybe having a pint with his old friend would provide the distraction they both needed.

Merrick answered his phone immediately. Sam thought he sounded weary.

'Hi stranger, long time no see,' he started breezily.

'Oh, it's you, Sam. I've been meaning

to ring, but . . . '

'I know . . . pressure of work.' Sam smiled into the phone. 'Do you think you could squeeze half an hour out of your busy day to have a pint with me?'

There was a slight hesitation at the other end and he wondered if Merrick was searching for a reason to refuse, but he said, 'Why not? I'd like that. What about the Red Lion, around five?'

The arrangement made, Sam clicked off the connection, shifting his stare back to the heap of witness statements.

His two DCs, Carter and Fox, and DS Will Tregellis were the key players in his team, but right now they looked as disheartened as he felt. He shuffled the papers, gathering them into a bundle, and marched through the office, dumping the lot on Will's desk.

'Divide these out,' he instructed. 'I want every single one going over again.' He heard the other two groan, and swung round to frown at them. 'And I want some results this time.'

He could feel three pairs of eyes on his back as he returned to his desk. He sat there going over in his head everything he knew about their victim. Priddy had confirmed Loveday's story that he had left his cottage to the Newlyn Fishermen's Federation. He'd heard of it, and by all accounts it did some excellent work supporting retired fishermen. It was a good cause, but why had Jago been so generous?

Sam went online and Googled the name. A basic webpage appeared on the screen. The organization had been set up ten years earlier by a group of Newlyn fishermen. It was a registered charity now, financed mainly by fundraising events and bequests like Jago's. It listed the kind of help it had given beneficiaries in the past — mostly cash donations and providing essential household equipment.

The secretary was named as Ray Penrose. There was a picture of him beside a boat in Newlyn Harbour. Sam studied the burly frame, the ruddy, weather-beaten face, stern blue eyes, and the bushy brown hair. Photographs could be deceptive, but to Sam's eyes, Mr Penrose didn't look like a man you would argue with.

He punched the contact number into

his phone. The voice that answered was gruff and sounded short-tempered. Sam could hear the sounds of a busy quayside in the background. The conversation was brief and to the point. Ray Penrose agreed to meet him at the harbour the next morning.

Sam replaced the phone thoughtfully. What they really needed were those PM results. He needed to speed things up.

* * *

'Okay, don't tell me.' The pathologist held up his hand as Sam walked into his office. 'You want to know how our friend died. And, as usual, you want all the details *yesterday*.'

Sam grinned.

'You know me so well, Robert.'

'And you know I can't tell you until it has been confirmed.'

'Not officially, perhaps. I understand that. I just need something . . . ' Sam gave him an appealing look.

Dr Bartholomew's bushy grey eyebrows shot up.

'Sounds more like you need something more significant than just *anything*.' He was pursing his lips, weighing up how much he could say. He trusted Sam. If the official lab results turned out to contradict his current opinion, he knew there would never be an accusing finger pointing at him.

'Okay.' He leaned back again. 'But you realize that this is just my initial summary.'

Sam nodded.

'There was definite bruising on the victim's arms. He was wearing a thin shirt, so the marks are quite clear . . . four points of contact on the back of each upper arm and one on the front of each arm.' He glanced up to the open door, and called out, 'Peter? Can you bring those photographs through?'

His ginger-haired assistant appeared in seconds, clutching a batch of photographs, and handed them to the pathologist.

Bartholomew thanked him and spread the photos out on the desk, and then pushed them across to Sam.

'You can see what I mean, here.' Sam did. The marks on Jago Tilley's arms suggested that someone had grabbed him from the front. He frowned at the picture.

'So he could have struggled with someone at the top of the stairs . . . and just lost his balance?'

'Maybe . . . ' Dr Bartholomew pursed his lips again. 'But I doubt if he could have bashed himself on the head like this.' He put another, more gruesome, image in front of Sam. 'I'd be looking for something like an iron bar to cause that damage.'

The sight of Jago Tilley's brutally battered head made Sam wince. He looked up quickly. 'So what about the streaks of blood at the top of the stairs?'

The pathologist turned the photograph back to himself and traced a finger over it. He said, 'There were flakes of paint in this other facial wound, and blood on the victim's hands. Looks like he struck his head on the wall at the top of the landing and then put his hands to the wound.'

Sam shook his head, imagining Jago's frantic grabs to save himself as he hurtled down those stairs.

He tried to picture the attacker. Had they panicked, or had they stood calmly over the old man before battering him to death?

'So it *is* murder,' Will said later when Sam repeated the details of his meeting with the pathologist. He could hear the excitement in his voice.

'Yes, that's definite now,' Sam said. They had been unofficially treating it as murder all along, but it helped to get the confirmation. 'I'm heading back to the scene,' he added. 'Tell Amanda to meet me there. And I want you, Will, to get uniform out looking for that murder weapon.'

★　★　★

Sam glanced across at Loveday's cottage as he drove along the front in Marazion. It was a reflex action because he knew she wouldn't be there. She'd be back at her office in Truro.

He drove on, turning down into the terrace, and nodded his thanks to the young PC who lifted the tape to let him through. Parking, he got out and walked past the crime scene to tap on Priddy Rodda's door.

She gave him a wary look. 'Has something else happened?

'No, not at all. I actually came to ask for your help, Mrs Rodda.' His voice faltered a little. He didn't want a refusal. 'I wonder if you would come back to Jago's cottage with me? I know we've already done this, but sometimes it's helpful to go over things again.'

Priddy frowned. She didn't relish going back into Jago's house, not when she couldn't get the sight of him lying there at the foot of his stairs out of her mind. But the big, handsome detective was smiling at her in such a persuasive way that she could hardly refuse.

The front door of the cottage was open, and Sam poked his head in. The Scene of Crime team had been told to take another look at the premises because the initial examination had turned up so little evidence.

A young woman, dressed in the obligatory white paper suit, was carefully scraping flakes of paint from the bannister. She glanced round and straightened up when she recognized the new arrival.

Sam raised an eyebrow at her and she nodded.

'Yes, sir. It's fine. We're pretty much finished in here now.'

Priddy glanced around the cottage in dismay. Carpets had been lifted, drawers turned out, floorboards ripped up.

'Why did they have to make such a mess?' she said. 'Whatever else they said about Jago, he was always tidy. He'll be looking down on all this right now, and cursing.'

'I'm sorry,' Sam said. 'But I'm afraid all this is necessary. I'm sure they will do their best to tidy up before they go.' He swallowed and glanced away, for he was sure that would *not* happen. They were standing in the gloomy front room, which now looked gloomier than ever.

'I know it's difficult, but could you just have another look around and tell me if you notice anything missing?'

It was a long shot, but they didn't have many options.

'Well, if you think it will help,' Priddy said uncertainly, trying to stop her eyes straying back to the spot at the bottom of the stairs where Jago's blood was still on the carpet.

She forced herself to concentrate, taking a slow look around the room, and shook her head.

'I'm sorry, Inspector . . . there's nothing.'

Sam's eyes were on the patch on the wall.

'And you're sure you can't remember what happened to the picture that used to hang here?'

'I don't remember, Inspector, because I never knew in the first place.'

She was staring at the fireplace, frowning.

'There is something missing, though.'

Sam felt his gut clenching.

She pointed to the right side of the fender.

'The poker . . . it's gone.'

Sam's mind was racing. Bartholomew had described the murder weapon as possibly an iron bar. Could a poker be an iron bar? It would do in his book.

He stepped outside to ring Will, when Amanda's car pulled up behind his own.

'Tell the search team we could be looking for a poker,' he said into his phone.

'Like this, you mean, sir?'

Sam wheeled round. The young forensic officer was holding up what looked like a bloodstained poker that had been sealed in a plastic evidence bag.

'We had another dig around that coal bunker out back.' She gave an apologetic frown. 'We dug a little deeper this time.'

Sam stared at the poker. It was the first real break they'd had. He beckoned Priddy forward.

'Is this Jago's poker?'

Priddy's eyes widened in horror, and her hand flew to her mouth.

She nodded, her voice shaking.

'That's it,' she said.

Confident that they had found the murder weapon, Sam left Amanda to finish up with the forensics team, and drove back to the station feeling slightly more optimistic about the case than he had done all day. There wasn't a lot more they could do until the lab results on the poker came through, hopefully in the morning.

It was just before five when Sam left

the station and crossed the road, threading his way through the back streets to the pub.

Christmas was now less than two weeks away and he still hadn't bought any presents for Jack and Maddie. No doubt Victoria's new bloke would be more organized. He felt his jaw tighten at the thought of how much access the man had to his children. Loveday was right, he had to make a greater effort to get up to Plymouth more often.

Victoria had met Matt Reeves at a singles club and they had hit it off at once, or so she'd told him. Sam wanted his family to be happy. It wasn't the kids' fault that he had split up with their mother. It wasn't Victoria's either, for that matter. The blame lay squarely on his shoulders. The job played such a big part in his life that he hardly saw Jack and Maddie growing up.

And then he'd lost Tessa. It was more than four years since she had died under the wheels of a car. The driver had been drinking. At the time Sam thought that he too would die of grief, but then he met

Loveday — and he hadn't died.

When Loveday came along, he'd fought against getting involved again, but she'd been hard to resist. He loved her independent streak, her energy and her sense of justice. He didn't always approve of her knack for getting involved in his cases, which was what had sparked this latest fall-out. She'd told him their relationship was over. So why didn't it feel like that?

Merrick was standing at the bar of the Red Lion when Sam walked in. He crossed the floor and put a hand on his friend's shoulder.

'Long time, no see.'

Merrick swung round.

'Hey, Sam.' He was trying to sound bright, but he wasn't fooling anyone. 'Shouldn't you be off catching criminals?'

Two other drinkers at the bar glanced in Sam's direction.

'I got time off for good behaviour.' Sam grinned, nodding to the corner table by the fire. 'Let's grab a seat over there.'

The landlord had made an effort to give the pub a festive air. Fairy lights were strung across the bar, and a small

116

Christmas tree twinkled blue and silver from across the room. Garlands of fake greenery were draped across the shelf above the fire, and bunches of red baubles hung from the pub's old oak beams.

A pint of frothy beer was slid along the counter to him and he picked it up, following Merrick to the table.

'So,' said Sam, studying his friend's serious face. 'Do you want to talk about it?'

Merrick positioned his glass on the stained beermat in front of him, and sat back with a resigned sigh.

'No beating about the bush, eh, Sam? Has someone put you up to this?'

Sam saw no point in lying.

'Loveday's worried about you.'

Merrick smiled.

'Ah, Loveday. Yes, she does worry, doesn't she?'

'Is she right to worry?'

Merrick was silent for so long that Sam didn't think he was going to answer. But then he said, 'Cadan's back.'

Sam nodded.

Merrick stared at him. 'You already

knew, didn't you . . . but how? Have you seen him?'

'Eh, no, actually. Not me.' He paused. 'It was Loveday who saw him . . . in the office.'

Merrick looked shocked.

'Loveday saw my brother in my office?'

'On the top floor, where you keep the old files. He was searching for something.'

Sam could see the questions scrolling through Merrick's mind.

'When was this?'

'Yesterday. Look, Merrick, are you going to tell me what's going on?'

Merrick ran the tip of his tongue over dry lips and took a moment before answering.

'Cadan is trying to take the magazine off me.'

Sam stared at him. 'What! He can't do that . . . can he?'

'I'm not sure. He's claiming there was a legal flaw in the original documents drawn up when the old man turned the business over to me.'

'What sort of flaw?'

'Oh, God knows. The papers are

couched in so much legal gobbledygook that he could be right.' He pushed a hand through his greying hair. 'I didn't understand any of it.'

'What happens if he's right?'

'If he's right, and the business really is his . . . well, we can say goodbye to *Cornish Folk*. Cadan doesn't want the magazine, he only wants the money he'd get if he sold it.'

Sam wasn't looking forward to explaining all this to Loveday. If Merrick lost the magazine it would destroy him. And Loveday might not even stay on in Cornwall, not when he knew other magazines were after her. He narrowed his eyes, thinking.

'It still doesn't explain what your brother was doing rifling through the files.'

'No,' Merrick said slowly. 'It doesn't, does it.'

'So what are you going to do about it?'

Merrick spread his hands in a gesture of helplessness.

'What can I do? Until I hear from Oliver Kilpatrick, the company solicitor, my hands are tied.'

'Where is Cadan now?' Sam asked.

'How would I know? He's probably back at the house.' Merrick gave a long, laboured sigh. 'He's moved back in — and probably at this very minute trying to wheedle his way into the old man's affections.'

Sam caught sight of the clock and threw back the remains of his pint.

'I'm sorry, Merrick. We're in the middle of this murder inquiry, and — '

Merrick didn't let him finish the sentence. He put up his hand. 'I know. You have to get back. It was good of you to think about me.'

'Would you like me to have a word with Cadan?' Sam said.

The look of alarm in Merrick's face startled Sam.

'No . . . there's no need for you to speak to Cadan. I'll handle this myself.'

Sam narrowed his eyes. 'Is there something else that you're not telling me, Merrick?'

'Of course not. It's just . . . Look, Sam, I know you're only trying to help, and I really appreciate your support, but it's nothing to worry about . . . really it's not. I'll sort it.'

Sam wasn't so sure about that. But if Merrick didn't want his help, he could hardly force it on him. They got up and left the pub together, pausing on the pavement.

Sam turned to Merrick.

'Don't tell Loveday I mentioned her name, will you? We're not exactly . . . ' He frowned. ' . . . getting on great at the moment.'

Merrick gave Sam a grim smile and put a hand on his shoulder.

'Maybe it should have been *me* listening to *your* problems.'

7

Something had been bothering Loveday all afternoon. It was something about her visit to Morvah that she couldn't quite put a finger on. Stressing about it was useless; forcing the issue would only succeed in pushing it further away. It would come to her in time; she'd just have to be patient.

She had just slid a chicken breast under the grill when she heard the car draw up, and went to the door.

'Sam!'

'Not an inconvenient time, I hope?' His nose twitched. 'You're cooking. I should have called first.'

'Come in.' She turned away, leaving him to follow her. 'It's only chicken, and I can always stick another piece under the grill if you want to join me.'

'I didn't come to be fed.' He came into the kitchen. 'But if you're offering . . . ' He folded his arms and leaned against the worktop in the casual way that was so familiar to her.

Sam had toyed with the idea of bringing a bottle, but decided it would have been too presumptuous, although of what exactly he wasn't sure. It wasn't strictly a social call. He wanted to tell her about his chat with Merrick, but he waited until they had eaten and had carried their mugs of coffee through to the fire in Loveday's tiny sitting-room.

He glanced round the cosy space, realizing that over the past couple of years he had probably spent as much time here as he had at his own place in Stithians.

It was Loveday who brought the subject up first.

'So, Sam, I'm presuming you've had a word with Merrick?' She raised an eyebrow. 'Did you find out what's wrong with him?'

He paused before answering, and she hoped he wasn't going to tell her that Merrick was ill. But that wasn't it.

'It seems you were right, Loveday. There is a problem — and it does concern Cadan.'

Sam described his conversation with Merrick in detail, including the bit when he'd told him how Loveday had found his brother in the magazine offices on Sunday, searching through old files.

He'd been undecided whether or not to confess that he'd mentioned Loveday's involvement, but had come to the conclusion there was no way he could have kept her out of it.

Loveday leaned forward. 'What did Merrick say?'

'He wasn't happy.' Sam saw her wince, and quickly put up a hand. 'Not about you. It's Cadan that's blotted his copybook. Apparently, he's come back to Cornwall with some idea of — ' He glanced at her. ' — taking over the magazine.'

She stared at him.

'Taking over the magazine? He can't do that.'

Sam shrugged.

'Merrick's not sure, but he's taking the thing seriously enough to have involved the firm's lawyer. Cadan is claiming there was a mistake made in the legal documents when old man Tremayne transferred the business to Merrick.'

Loveday didn't like the sound of this. She got up, heading for the kitchen where there was the best part of a bottle of Pinot Grigio in the fridge. She brought it back with two glasses.

If the magazine fell into Cadan's hands, there was no way he would keep it on. He would sell it to the highest bidder, and she and all the others would be out of a job. But it wasn't herself she was worried about right now. The publication was Merrick's life. He'd made so many sacrifices to keep it going, and at last the circulation was beginning to climb. Loveday hoped her own efforts had something to do with that.

Sam stood up and took the glasses and bottle from her as she sank thoughtfully onto her chair.

'Merrick must have thought it possible that Cadan has a claim, or he wouldn't have involved Oliver Kilpatrick,' she said, her mind snapping back to earlier that day at the Tremayne house when Cadan had gone off to take his phone call as she was leaving. She remembered his eyes. He had definitely been troubled. And then Connie running after her like that and telling her about Rupert Caine. She glanced up at Sam and repeated the name.

'Have you ever heard of him?'

Sam frowned, trying to remember. Then he nodded. Of course . . . Rupert Caine Classic Cars. That's why the name had been familiar. He was a very successful businessman with showrooms mainly in Devon. As far as he knew, the man was a pillar of the community. He told Loveday what he knew.

'I suppose it's possible that Cadan bought a car from him, and then couldn't finance the payments. But I can't see Rupert Caine employing heavies to put the frighteners on his bad debtors. As far as I know, he's pretty straight.'

Loveday's eyes sparked with excitement.

'Did you know that he has a son of the same name? Although he calls himself Rupe Caine.'

Sam nodded.

'Vaguely. But isn't he in Las Vegas?'
Loveday nodded.

'He used to be. I Googled him and he's now living in Plymouth, where he runs . . . wait for it . . . a casino.'

She was watching Sam's face, smiling when she saw the reaction she'd been hoping for.

Sam's eyes narrowed.

'Now I remember. Young Caine had a reputation that reached all the way across the Atlantic. His old man set him up in business over there to get him out of the way. He'd got himself involved with London gangsters.' He frowned. 'You think it's this Caine that Cadan's got himself involved with?'

'It would make sense,' Loveday said, reaching for the glass of wine Sam had poured, and taking a sip of the cold liquid. 'I don't know if Cadan's a gambling man, but it wouldn't surprise me. And just supposing he'd got himself in a bit deeper than he'd planned, and got landed with some serious debt, well . . . '
She leaned back in her chair, glass in hand. 'This Rupe character doesn't sound

like the kind of man you would want to owe money to.'

She glanced across at Sam, who had made himself comfortable in the chair opposite, and continued, 'It all fits. If Cadan owes money to this character then he's going to be desperate enough to clutch at straws, maybe even be prepared to do a bit of dodgy dealing of his own.'

Sam put up a hand.

'Hang on. Let's not get ahead of ourselves.'

'But it is all possible, isn't it?' She could feel a spark of excitement growing inside her.

'Of course it is,' he said, draining his glass and getting to his feet. 'And I promise I'll look into it.'

He hesitated for a moment, looking down at her, giving her the opportunity to tell him to stay, but she didn't. Not that he had actually expected it. Not all the bridges had been rebuilt between them, but maybe they were getting there.

Loveday also got up and followed him to the door. As he turned to say goodnight, she stretched up and kissed him on the cheek.

'Goodnight, Sam . . . and thanks.'

Sam gazed down at her for a moment, and then nodded.

She watched his car move up the drive. It had begun to snow again. She could see the flakes drifting across the beam of his headlights.

She closed the door quietly and turned back to the warmth of her sitting-room — and then stopped. Something had suddenly clicked in her head. Her eyes lit up. She now knew what it was she had been trying to remember. It was about Sabine De Fries. Hadn't there been talk in her friend's circle about Sabine bailing out a boyfriend who had gambling debts?

At the time it had seemed unlikely, given that the ice-cool blonde had appeared too much of a high flier to get herself involved with a loser. But what if that gambling man was Cadan? It was certainly one theory, but right now it was a theory so full of holes and improbabilities that it would need a lot of thinking about.

She lay in bed that night wondering if

she should share her suspicions with Sam, but they were so flimsy that he was bound to dismiss them as fanciful. Maybe they were, but she knew with certainty that if they proved to be true, then she would have to warn Sabine about Cadan Tremayne.

★ ★ ★

Loveday tapped lightly on Cassie's kitchen door as she left for work next morning, but it was Adam who opened it. Behind him she could hear Sophie and Leo squabbling, and her friend's increasingly harassed voice, trying to calm them down. She frowned. Now was not the time for neighbourly chat.

'It's all right, Cassie,' she called. 'I'm not stopping. I just wanted to . . . '

She didn't get a chance to finish the sentence, for Cassie had appeared at Adam's shoulder.

'Wanted what . . . ?'

'It's okay, I can see you've got your hands full. I'll give you a ring later.'

Cassie shot a glance back to the

children. The squealing had stopped, and Adam had gone back to dishing out breakfast cereals.

'See . . . ' She gave a wry smile. 'He's wasted as a GP. He should have been a professional childminder. He's so much better at this than me.' She turned back to her friend. 'So what did you want, Loveday?'

'Jago's funeral. It's today, isn't it? I just wondered what time.'

Cassie sighed. 'There was a bit of a hitch there. I think Priddy was being a tad optimistic when she gave everybody that information. The body's only being released to the family today — well, released to Priddy, actually. Poor old Jago had no family, except for the useless Billy Travis, and he won't be going out of his way to help.'

Loveday frowned. 'I didn't realize that. So when will it be?'

'Tomorrow at eleven, here in the town church. I expect it will be a full house. Old Jago was popular. I've promised Priddy I'll be there, but I could really do without this at the moment. Is that awful of me?' She pushed her fingers through her blonde hair. 'We're absolutely snowed under at the agency. I've taken on two new contracts to refurbish yachts in Falmouth Marina, and now I'm wondering how we are going to fit them into the pre-Christmas schedule.'

Loveday nodded.

'I know exactly how you feel. I have two interviews lined up for today, and another for the morning, never mind the stuff piling up in my in-tray. I really need to get it all sorted out, or else I would have come with you. I feel quite guilty about not being there.'

Cassie took her friend's arm and walked her to her car.

'You didn't even know the man, so there's nothing for you to feel guilty about.'

Loveday glanced out across the bay, to where a watery sun was trying to break through the cloud base. It didn't lift her spirits. 'I suppose I just feel . . . involved,' she said.

'I'll give you a ring after the funeral and let you know how it's all gone. How would that do?'

Loveday smiled.

'Thanks, Cassie.' She opened the car door and slid in behind the wheel. 'Tell Priddy I'll be thinking about her,' she called back as she pulled away.

The magazine's complicated publication schedules meant they were working on the March edition. The December issue, currently in the shops, had been done and dusted three months previously. Only those people who were not involved in the production of magazines thought the timescales strange.

It was all very different from Loveday's time as a newspaper reporter in Glasgow, where immediacy was everything. Stories she wrote one day would appear in the next day's paper, or even in specially-produced editions the same day if the story was important enough. She gave a wry smile. Things were a bit more laid-back in Cornwall.

⋆ ⋆ ⋆

The 'Murder Wall', as the CID team referred to their whiteboard, was filling

133

up fast. There were several pictures of the crime scene, most depicting the poor bruised body of Jago Tilley, together with a photograph of the bloodstained poker that had been recovered from the old man's coal bunker. There was a head-and-shoulders mugshot of Billy Travis. Priddy Rodda's picture was there, too, along with a printout of the home page of the Newlyn Fishermen's Federation website. Shots of the front and back of Jago's cottage, with pointed-out access to both town centre and beach. And there was a hand-drawn sketch of the area, tracking the distance from the pub to the crime scene.

'How are we doing with those witness statements, Amanda?' Sam asked, as his team of officers gathered for their morning briefing.

'We're still trying to contact the owners of one of the neighbouring properties, in Canada, sir. But I have spoken to the people on the other side, who live in London. Apparently they've only met the victim once or twice.

'And as for the pub customers . . . ' She

sighed. 'We've checked and double-checked their statements, but we still haven't come up with anything new.' Amanda's mind went back to the Five Stars Inn, and the morning they'd spent questioning the locals.

'We could try speaking to one old guy again, though.' She reached across her desk for the bundle of statements and flicked through them until she found the one she wanted. 'Here he is, Harry Tasker. He was our victim's best mate, and he was definitely the most upset.' She handed the sheets to Sam. 'But my money's still on the nephew, sir, even if he does have an alibi.'

Sam took the sheet and gave it a cursory glance. 'According to this Mr Tasker's statement, he left the pub before Jago.'

Amanda nodded.

'I suppose this was confirmed by other customers in the pub?'

'It was, sir.'

Sam sighed. 'I think we need another word with him. I'll go down there myself.'

He was aware of Amanda's frown. No

doubt she felt he was pulling rank by not trusting her to take the second interview, but it wasn't that. If Harry Tasker was Jago's best mate there would be things he knew about the old man, things that perhaps only he did.

A mobile incident room had been set up at the top of the terrace, and door-to-door enquiries were still taking place throughout the town.

Sam glanced at Will.

'What about that murder weapon?'

'Being checked out as we speak.'

'Give forensics a ring and chivvy them on,' Sam said, switching his attention to Malcolm Carter. 'What do we know about Billy Travis's associates?'

'He fenced some pictures to a dodgy art dealer in St Ives . . . a Zachariah Paxton-Quinn, would you believe?'

A snigger went round the room at the man's name.

'So what do we have on this man?'

'Nothing specific. We've had him in for questioning a few times when he's been reported selling stolen goods, but he always manages to slip under the net.'

'Okay, Malcolm,' Sam said, grabbing his coat. 'Let's go see what Mr Paxton-Quinn's got to say for himself.'

★　★　★

St Ives was like a ghost town on the cold December morning. Sam and Malcolm had no trouble parking on the front. The sharp tang of salty air hit them as they got out of the car and walked along the deserted seafront. The tide was in and the water was slapping high against the sea wall.

They carried on towards the lifeboat house, stopping by the stylish chrome and black frontage of Zachariah Paxton-Quinn's gallery, and paused to look at the paintings on display in the window. Malcolm tilted his head and narrowed his eyes at the colour-splattered canvases.

'What the hell is this supposed to be? My dog could do better than that,' he said.

Sam smiled.

'Some people like it.' He was thinking of Loveday's artist friends.

Malcolm made a face. 'What happened to Cornish coves and old fishing boats?'

These paintings weren't Sam's cup of tea either. He much preferred a good seascape, or even a picture of the bleak, windswept moors with the chimney of an old tin mine in the distance.

Sam's attention was already on the gallery's interior as he preceded Malcolm into the shop. His eye was caught by a large floor-to-ceiling exhibit on which the artist appeared to have daubed blocks of paint and simply allowed the colours to run into each other. He was still studying it when the man appeared from the back of the gallery.

Sam took in the tall, wiry frame and crinkly brown hair that fell to just short of the man's shoulders. His dark red silk shirt was tucked into tight-fitting jeans and there was arrogance in the assessing dark eyes and sharply-chiselled features.

'Please feel free to browse, gentlemen.' He gave them his professional smile. 'And if there is anything I can help you with, you only have to ask.'

Sam guessed him to be in his

mid-fifties, although he looked younger. His voice was smooth, the tone careful and well modulated. It was difficult to place the accent. 'We were looking for Mr Paxton-Quinn.'

The dark eyes turned wary.

'And you are?'

Sam took out his warrant card. 'Detective Inspector Kitto.' He inclined his head towards Malcolm, who was also displaying his ID. 'And this is Detective Constable Carter. Could we have a word, sir?'

Zachariah Paxton-Quinn's thin lips pursed and he gave an irritated frown.

'A word about what?'

'We understand that you are a friend of Billy Travis?'

The man's eyes flickered only a fraction.

'Then you understand wrong, Inspector.'

'You don't know Billy Travis?' Sam said.

'Never heard of him.'

'Oh, come on, Mr Quinn. We *know* that you know him,' said Malcolm.

The man gave him a sharp look.

'I repeat, I've never heard of this person. Should I have?'

Sam rolled his eyes to the ceiling. 'We don't have time for this. Now either you can tell us the truth, Mr Quinn, or we take you down to the station.' He gave a laboured sigh. 'So I'll ask again. Tell us about your involvement with Billy Travis.'

The man glanced away, but not before Sam caught the glint of panic in the dark eyes.

'Okay,' he conceded reluctantly. 'I know him, but I'm not involved in any of his scams. What's he done, anyway?'

'His uncle was murdered three days ago,' Malcolm cut in.

Paxton-Quinn shrugged.

'I don't see what that has to do with me.'

'Well, that's what we're here to find out.' Malcolm continued, 'You see, if you were acquainted with Billy, then perhaps you also knew his uncle, Jago Tilley?'

Sam was holding back, letting Malcolm shoot the questions while he studied the man. He could see the dark shadow of guilt in his eyes and knew he was lying. The narrow shoulders lifted in a shrug. 'I've never heard of Mr Tilley. I'll hold up my hands to having met Travis, but I know nothing of his family . . . and I certainly don't know about any murder.'

'Exactly how do you know Billy Travis?' Sam said.

There was a pause, and Sam could see Quinn's mind working as he decided how much to tell them.

'He comes into the gallery now and again.'

Malcolm allowed his gaze to travel over the artwork on display.

'Billy Travis buys this stuff? Is that what you're telling us?'

Sam gave a patient sigh.

'We have a big computer in our office, Mr Quinn, and your name features on it quite a bit. So if you're not prepared to be straight with us right now, we can do this back at the station in Truro.'

'Okay . . . okay.' The man put up his hands. 'I bought stuff from him now and again. Nothing stolen, mind you . . . at least that's what he told me.'

Sam shook his head.

'And you believed him, of course.' He narrowed his eyes at the man. 'What kind of stuff', Mr Quinn?'

'Little bits of porcelain, collectables, Clarice Cliff, Troika . . . stuff like that. I deal in antiques as well as art.'

Sam frowned.

'Has he ever brought pictures to you?'

'You mean paintings? No, never.'

'No, I didn't mean paintings. I said pictures . . . in particular, a drawing . . . a sketch of a woman?'

Out of the corner of his eye he could see Malcolm glancing at him. He hadn't really worked out for himself yet what was in his mind. The missing picture was still bugging him. It was possible that Travis had taken it from Jago's cottage. But why would that be of any interest to him? Unless it was valuable, which was most unlikely.

Sam saw Paxton-Quinn's attention flick to the gallery door and then immediately glance away. He spun round in time to catch the back view of a woman who, on seeing Sam and Malcolm, had turned on her heel and hurried away.

'We seem to be frightening off your customers, Mr Quinn,' Sam said solemnly, his eyes still on the retreating figure.

The man flashed his much-practised, professional smile.

'I wouldn't worry about it, Inspector. I'm sure the lady would merely have been window-shopping. Most of my calling customers don't actually make any purchases. I earn my crust from my much more discerning clients.'

He held Sam's gaze for a few more seconds before looking away. He was wondering if he'd said enough to satisfy the detectives.

Sam took another glance out along the seafront, but the woman was no longer in sight.

'Okay, Mr Quinn. That'll be all for now. We may need to speak to you again.'

He could see the relief in the man's face as they left.

Outside the gallery the two officers headed back to the car. Apart from a couple of vehicles illegally parked on double yellow lines, the seafront was deserted.

Malcolm jerked his head back at the gallery.

'D'you think he knew her, sir?'

Sam squinted out across the steely grey water.

'I'm sure he did. What I don't yet know is why she took off like that.'

8

Sam checked his watch. It was almost noon. If they took the back road to Marazion they could be there in half an hour.

'Come on, Malcolm. I'll buy you a pint,' he said, heading back to the car.

There were three people standing at the bar in the Five Stars Inn when they arrived, and none of them looked old enough to be Harry Tasker.

Sam ordered a beer for Malcolm and an orange juice for himself, and the two officers stood at the bar supping their drinks. Sam caught the young barman's eye. 'No Harry Tasker today?' he asked.

The barman frowned. 'No, he's hardly been in since . . . '

The man beside Sam sighed and put down his beer glass. 'Old Harry's missing his mate Jago. It's hit him hard, poor old sod.'

The barman said, 'Are you the law?'

Sam and Malcolm reached into their jacket pockets for their warrant cards and the others nodded.

'Where can we find Mr Tasker?' Sam asked.

'He's not in any trouble, is he?' the barman asked. 'I mean, you don't think he had anything to do with Jago's death? He left here well before Jago that night.'

Sam wondered why the man should think that made Tasker's possible involvement with the murder any less likely.

He smiled. 'We only want to have a word with him.' He looked up, studying the young barman's face. His mind scrolled through the list of witness statements. He remembered the man's comments that Jago and Harry had been inseparable.

'I understand that the two were great friends,' he said.

The barman nodded towards the two stools at the end of the bar. 'That was their corner. They sat there holding court most nights.' He smiled, shaking his head. 'A couple of old codgers. Nobody could scrounge drinks like Jago and Harry.'

'You sound as though you liked them,' Sam said.

The barman nodded. 'Everybody did.'

'So where can we find Mr Tasker?'

'Most probably at home, I should think,' said Sam's neighbour at the bar. 'Shell Cottage. Walk up the hill on the main road and take the first turning on the left. It's the one with the green door.'

It wasn't difficult to see where the cottage got its name. Windows and door were framed in shells embedded into the plaster. They also lined the short path and topped the low wall that ran along the front of the house. The door was opened on Sam's first knock.

'I saw you coming up the hill,' Harry Tasker said, shuffling aside to allow the officers to duck through the low door.

He followed them into a very small, dark front room, where ashes from a glowing coal fire had spilled onto the stone hearth. Sam glanced around the messy space. There was no sign of a Mrs Tasker. He tried not to sigh at the sad scene. The room was littered with dirty cups and glasses, plates of unfinished

147

food and crumpled newspapers. Sam's eye fell on a copy of that day's *Western Morning News* that lay open at a page showing a report that police were now treating Jago's death as murder.

'Coppers, aren't you?' Harry scowled at them. 'Well I don't know nothing, except that Jago ain't coming back.'

Sam and Malcolm had brought out their IDs and were now replacing them in their jackets.

'I'm very sorry for your loss, Mr Tasker. I understand that you and Mr Tilley were good friends.'

'You could say that. Known each other since we were lads, we have.' Harry's voice came out in a smokey rasp. 'I used to crew for him when he had the boat.' The old grey eyes misted. 'Them were the days. We sailed out o' Newlyn . . . used to bump along that road in Jago's old truck, the fishing gear piled high in the back.'

'Did Jago's nephew ever sail with you?' Sam asked.

Harry's mouth curled in disgust. 'Oh, that one. He had no respect for Jago, and it was mutual. Billy Travis was round there all the time, mooching about for what he could get. He was always trying to tap Jago for a sub . . . wanted 'im to sell some o' his stuff, he did.'

'What stuff was that, Harry?' Malcolm cut in.

Harry shrugged. 'Don't know. Jago never said. As far as he knew, there was nothing valuable in his cottage.'

'You left the Five Stars early the night Jago died. Why was that, Harry?' Sam asked.

The old man's mouth was working as he stared into the embers of the fire. 'I'd had enough, that's why. I know me limits and we had been hitting it hard that night. Never could mix me beer and the rum.'

'Was Jago drinking more than usual as well?'

'Dunno . . . I suppose he was. Like I said, we both had a skinful. I just knew when it was time to go home.'

Malcolm leaned forward. 'Think carefully, now Harry. Were there any strangers in the bar that night?'

Harry reached for the cigarettes on the

table beside him and screwed up his eyes against the smoke as he lit one. 'There was one bloke I didn't know . . . bought me a pint before Jago came in . . . long hair, dressed casual-like. I remember thinking he was a bit o' a ponce, but if he wanted to buy me a pint, who was I to bother about something like that.'

Sam's head came up sharply. 'Can you remember anything else about this man . . . colour of his hair . . . how old he was?'

The old man screwed up his eyes, trying to recall the scene in the pub that night.

Malcolm flashed an impatient look to Sam, but they both waited.

And then Harry said, 'His hair was brown and kind of crinkly-like. Couldn't have been a day under fifty, but dressed younger.' He glanced back at the detectives. 'You know the type — flash black leather jacket and tight jeans.'

'Did he speak to Jago?' Malcolm asked.

'No, he'd gone before Jago arrived. Well . . . no. Wait a minute. I don't think he had actually left. The bar was busy and a few folk were drinking with Jago and me. But I might at one point have seen this bloke at the far end o' the bar.'

Sam felt a buzz of excitement as they walked back to his car.

'He was describing our Mr Paxton-Quinn, wasn't he, boss?'

'My thoughts exactly. I think we should invite Mr Quinn along to the station for a chat.' Sam was already holding his mobile phone to his ear. 'I'll get uniform to bring him in,' he said with a grim smile.

* * *

Merrick wasn't in his office when Loveday got in next morning. She raised an eyebrow at Keri, who answered with a shrug. It was another out-of-character moment for him not to be first in the office.

Leaving scribbled instructions for Keri to book Mylor Ennis — to take the extra-wide shots they needed for an article about a new artisan bakery in Fowey — she headed out of the office on foot.

Her second interview of the morning, which Loveday hoped would result in a *Cornish Folk* special picture spread, was with an acclaimed art historian who was currently cataloguing the work of the Newlyn School of Painters at a gallery in Penzance.

Rebecca Monteith also worked as a volunteer in the Truro Cathedral gift shop, and she had said this was the only time in the current week when an interview might be possible. It wasn't ideal. Loveday wasn't relishing the thought of trying to conduct a snatched interview between customers. But it was better than nothing. She'd had to work under far more difficult circumstances when she was a reporter on the Glasgow newspaper.

Her colleagues in the city newsroom had thought her mad to give up her job and move down to the 'sticks', as they'd described Cornwall. It was fine for holidays, but no one actually wanted to live there, they'd said, not when London beckoned.

There had been a time when she might have agreed with them, but her roots were in Cornwall, just as much as her Cornish mother's were . . .

She was allowing her mind to wander when she desperately needed to concentrate on the interview ahead. She tried to picture what Rebecca Monteith would be like as she hurried along Lemon Street.

She'd sounded younger and livelier on the phone than the mental image Loveday had formed in her head of a rather staid and serious art historian. She had reached Boscawen Street, waiting impatiently on the pavement for a gap in the traffic so she could run through the narrow lane that would take her to the side of the cathedral.

Christmas shoppers hurried past, doing their mental checklists of the presents they had to buy, and the preparations still to be made for the big day. Loveday hoped it wasn't an indication of how busy the cathedral gift shop would be.

Truro was especially attractive at this time of year. The shops were full of seasonal sparkle, and fairy lights twinkled from the trees. Loveday longed to linger and soak up the atmosphere, but not today. She was already late for her appointment with Rebecca. As she approached the cathedral, the buzz of voices drifted out from the open doors. Rehearsals for a carol concert were in progress. Loveday couldn't help stopping to smile at the young singers as she made her way through the building to the gift shop.

Rebecca Monteith was an elegant, silver-haired woman in her late forties, who looked more like Loveday's idea of a successful businesswoman doing something in fashion than the dusty art historian she had imagined her to be.

At that moment Rebecca was lifting delicate glass tree ornaments from their display and slipping them into a bag for her customer. Loveday caught her attention and smiled. The woman gave a helpless shrug — a silent apology for how busy the gift shop was. Over the next half-hour, Loveday was able to grab only a few minutes of disjointed conversation with the woman before she had to attend to another customer.

'I'm so sorry,' Rebecca said eventually. It was an upper-class Edinburgh accent. 'This wasn't such a good idea. I'm afraid

I've wasted your time.'

Loveday shook her head. She wasn't ready to give up just yet, but she knew without even looking at her diary that the next few days were full-on.

'I don't suppose you work at the weekends?'

'Not as a rule,' Rebecca said. 'But I have arranged to put in a couple of hours at the gallery this Saturday.'

'If I promise not to take up too much of your time, could I maybe call by then?'

The meeting was arranged and Loveday headed back to the office, satisfied that she had at least salvaged something from the last hour.

It had been Loveday's plan to spend the afternoon transcribing her taped interviews, but the phones had rung almost non-stop. Even the calm, efficient Keri had got herself into a flap.

The last thing Loveday needed on a day like this was having to rejig the pages of the 'work in progress' edition of the magazine, and move what was to be one of the main features to twenty pages further back.

So it was late when she got home that night, and after a quick snack, it was all she could do to crawl, exhausted, into bed.

* * *

Loveday didn't normally get involved with advertising features, but the company she was calling on the next day was a big spender, and a contract with them could be crucial to the magazine. She was on her way back to the office after the meeting as her phone rang. She smiled when she saw Cassie's name, and then immediately frowned. Of course! Jago's funeral. She'd been so immersed in her own world that she had completely forgotten about it. She felt a rush of guilt.

'Hi Cassie.' She cleared her throat. 'How did the funeral go?'

'Really well, actually. The church was full,' Cassie said, and then paused. 'Sam was there.'

'Was he?' Loveday frowned, and then realized that he was bound to have turned up. He was probably scanning the faces of

156

the mourners for any signs of guilty consciences. 'How was Priddy?'

'That's why I'm ringing, Loveday. I need a favour. Jago's will is being read on Friday at a solicitor's office in Penzance. Apparently Priddy is one of the beneficiaries, so she's been asked to attend.' She hesitated. 'I was wondering if you would go with her?'

Loveday's mind raced through the rest of her week's schedule. It wouldn't be easy. She certainly couldn't cancel any of her appointments. On the other hand, this was a kind of emergency. She'd told Priddy she could depend on her if she needed any help. Maybe Keri could juggle her diary around?

'I would go myself,' Cassie was saying. 'But I'm so tied up with this new contract that I just don't see how I can get away.'

'No worries.' Loveday smiled into the phone. 'Of course I'll go with her. If you give me the details, I'll ring her now.'

Cassie let out a relieved sigh.

'Thanks, Loveday. I knew I could depend on you.' She dictated the address, and Loveday ducked into a shop doorway to jot the details down in her notebook.

'Priddy wants to make her own way into Penzance, so it would be just a case of meeting her at the solicitor's office.'

'Consider it done,' Loveday said.

★ ★ ★

Sam stared at his overflowing inbox, depressingly aware that he would have to deal with it at some point. His mind kept returning to that packed church in Marazion. Jago Tilley had been a popular man, but then if he'd lived in the town all his life he was bound to have known a lot of people.

It was about time they got a break in the case. It was the least Jago deserved.

He glanced at his watch. Paxton Quinn definitely had more to tell them, and Sam had asked uniform to bring him into the station. His phone rang and he snatched at it, anger flickering in his eyes as he listened to the caller.

'What do you mean, you can't find him? Keep looking!' He slammed the instrument down and cursed just as Will tapped his office door and poked his head round with an apologetic grimace. 'Bad time, boss?'

'Uniform have lost Paxton-Quinn.'

Will opened his mouth to speak, but Sam put up a hand. 'Don't ask. All they had to do was to pick him up and bring him here. Apparently Mr Quinn had other ideas and disappeared out the back door of the gallery while Cornwall's finest waited out front.'

'He won't have got far. We'll find him,' Will reasoned.

'We shouldn't have to, Will. He was right there and we let him wriggle away.'

'Of course, there's another way of looking at it,' Will said. 'I mean, sneaking away like that isn't something an innocent man would do.'

Sam got up and went to the window, staring down at the traffic, and then he wheeled round to face Will. 'Let's go find him.'

The two officers spent the rest of the day knocking on doors in St Ives. The town's artist community was a tightly-knit bunch who looked after their own, and no one was talking.

Most of the customers around the bar of the Harbour Inn looked like fishermen, and although a few of them admitted to knowing Paxton Quinn, none could shed any light on his current whereabouts.

But when they were leaving, the barman called them aside, saying he'd heard the man had a girlfriend in Hale, whose father ran an antiques shop on the front there.

It was dark when they got outside, and a chilling wind was tugging at the strings of fairy lights around the harbour.

'Where to now, boss — Hale?'

'Home,' Sam said wearily. 'I'm fed up chasing this joker all over Cornwall. We'll let uniform ferret him out tomorrow, and hope they do a better job this time.'

9

Sam drove back to Truro and dropped Will off at the station. He'd phoned in and was told there was nothing new to report, so he decided not to go up to his office. Facing a mounting pile of time-and-motion study reports was the last thing he felt like doing. He picked up his phone and punched in Loveday's number.

'Fancy eating out tonight?'

'What's the catch?' Loveday said, laughing.

'Absolutely none,' he replied. But they both knew that wasn't true; for if they chose to eat at the Godolphin in Marazion, there was every possibility he would end up staying the night.

'We could have something in Truro for a change,' he offered, and smiled when he heard the note of disappointment in Loveday's voice.

'Or we could just go to the Godolphin,' she suggested.

He grinned. 'You've twisted my arm. See you there about seven?'

'Fine by me,' she said.

That gave him an hour to spare, and he headed for his cottage in Stithians to shower and change.

His phone was tinkling as he came out of the bathroom wrapped in a towel. It was Victoria. He grabbed it. She didn't often ring him like this.

'Everything all right, Victoria?'

'Of course it is. Why do you always have to assume the worst? We're all fine; more than fine, actually.' She hesitated. 'That's what I wanted to talk to you about, Sam.'

He braced himself. 'Yes?'

'Well, the thing is, Sam . . . I'm taking Jack and Maddie away for Christmas.'

He waited. That was twice she'd called him 'Sam'. He knew he wasn't going to like whatever was coming next.

'The thing is . . . we're going to Florida.'

'Florida! You're going to Florida?' He hadn't even bought his kids' Christmas gifts yet, and they were going to Florida.

'But I was hoping to see Jack and Maddie over the Christmas holidays,' he protested. 'When are you going?'

'Saturday the twentieth, coming back the day after Boxing Day.'

Sam let out a low whistle. 'Have you won the lottery, Victoria? You can't afford that.'

There was silence at the other end of the line, and then Victoria said, 'Matt's paying. It's his Christmas gift to us.'

A slow pounding had started in Sam's head. His ex-wife's new boyfriend, Matt Reeves, was taking *his* children away for Christmas, and there wasn't a damn thing he could do about it.

'Didn't you think of consulting me before making this decision? I take it the children already know?'

'They're over the moon, Sam. Don't spoil it for them.'

She was right. He could hardly step in and act the heavy absentee father. But it hurt. It hurt like hell.

'It's still a week away.' Victoria was trying to sound reasonable. 'You've got plenty of time to see Jack and Maddie before we leave.'

But that was just it. He hadn't, not

when he was in the middle of a murder investigation. All the way to Marazion he tried to repress the thought of how this Matt person would be endearing himself to *his* kids over Christmas. The weasel would be lavishing money on Jack and Maddie in a way that he could never afford to.

Loveday knew something was wrong as soon as Sam walked into the Godolphin. Her heart did an alarming little flip as she went to meet him, linking arms and walking with him into the bar.

He ordered their drinks, and attempted a smile. She wondered if he was about to tell her that he'd decided to end their relationship after all.

She took a long swallow of her wine. 'Just say it right out, Sam . . . whatever it is. I'd rather you told me now than let it lie between us all night.'

Sam frowned. 'What on earth are you talking about, Loveday?'

'I'm talking about you, Sam. You look as though you've got the weight of the world on your shoulders. What's wrong with you?'

He lifted the pint he'd just been served. 'It's Jack and Maddie,' he said. Over the next half-hour Loveday listened as he retold the story, getting angrier with every second.

'Okay, Sam, so you're good and mad, and you've every right to be, but I don't see how you can stop them going.'

Sam grimaced at her. 'Is this supposed to make me feel better?'

'Of course not. But look — ' She reached out and took his hand. ' — you're just feeling raw inside right now, but you need to put yourself in Jack and Maddie's shoes. Going to Florida will be a wonderful adventure for them. They'll have a ball.'

'And he'll be paying for it,' Sam said bitterly.

'Well, let him. They'll still come back to you.'

They had hot food in front of them now, and from the window they could see the lights of St Michael's Mount glowing in the darkness. Sam sank back in his chair. 'I can't even get through to Plymouth to see them before they leave.'

'Couldn't they come here? They could maybe stay for a night. I'll muck in and look after them if you get called away.'

Sam frowned. He hadn't thought of that, but yes: the kids could come to Cornwall and he could spend a whole evening with them. Why not? He stretched across the table and planted a kiss on Loveday's mouth. 'I don't deserve you,' he said, smiling.

'You're right about that, but tell me later . . . ' She gave him a coy grin. ' . . . when we get home.'

* * *

It was early afternoon on Friday when Loveday drove up Market Jew Street looking for a parking space. She should have known better than to expect to find one here on a busy Friday, let alone this close to Christmas. The town was glittering with Yuletide cheer and Loveday's spirits rose as she negotiated the busy thoroughfare.

Penzance, with its quirky raised walkway running down one side of the main shopping street, and the imposing statue of Sir Humphry Davy, of the miners' lamp fame, looking down on it all, was one of Loveday's favourite places.

At the top of the hill she turned left into Chapel Street, and spotted Priddy at once. She was wearing a smart black coat and hat, and right at that moment was pacing the pavement, glancing anxiously in both directions. Loveday looked at the clock on her dashboard. She was ten minutes early. Priddy was obviously nervous.

The nearest parking space she could find was at the bottom of the road, opposite the red brick building where a plaque by the door informed passers-by that this was the house where Maria Branwell, mother of the Brontë sisters, had once lived.

Loveday felt her heartbeat quicken as she walked briskly back up the hill.

Priddy's face split into a relieved smile as soon as she spotted her, and hurried forward to meet her.

'It was so good of you to come. I . . . ' She glanced back at the solicitor's office. 'I hate these places. If you hadn't turned up I would have just walked away.'

But Loveday suspected she was remembering her last visit here with Jago. The past few days had been traumatic and the old lady was now feeling the strain. It was understandable. Loveday smiled and took her arm, guiding her through the glass door.

'This could be good news for you, Priddy. Jago has obviously left you something he wanted you to have.'

Priddy bit her lip.

'Do you think so?'

With a name like 'Cuthbert, Timms and Bodilly' above the door, Loveday had expected a dusty old office, but the place was smart and new-looking. The young blonde receptionist, who looked still in her late teens, glanced up with an enquiring smile.

'This lady is Mrs Priddy Rodda,' Loveday explained. 'And she has come to see Mr Timms.'

The girl indicated behind them.

'If you would take a seat with these gentlemen, Mr Timms will be out in just a moment.'

168

They both wheeled round, surprised to see two men sitting in an alcove not visible from the door. The one who looked like a big burly fisherman nodded to them. The other smaller one with the shaven head grimaced and looked away.

'That's Billy Travis,' Priddy said, in a stage whisper from the side of her mouth. And then she smiled. 'I might enjoy this after all.'

The burly man stood up and offered Priddy his hand.

'Ray Penrose, from the Newlyn Fishermen's Federation,' he said. 'You'll be Jago's neighbour.'

Priddy took his hand hesitantly.

'Has Jago mentioned me to you?'

'Once or twice,' the man said, grinning.

At that moment a tall, lively-looking young man with a mop of curly black hair strode towards them, smiling.

'I'm Rodney Timms,' he announced, shaking hands with each of the four of them in turn. 'Please come into my office.'

Loveday hesitated, wondering if she should follow them through. The reading of Jago Tilley's will was officially nothing to do with her. But Priddy caught her arm and glanced up at the solicitor.

'I want my friend to come in with me. Is that all right?'

Rodney Timms glanced at the two men. The fisherman smiled and nodded. Billy Travis's shoulders went up in a 'don't care' shrug.

The office had a huge window that looked out onto the street. Three ladder-backed chairs had been arranged in a row opposite the solicitor's desk, and he took another one from the corner of the room for Loveday. When they were all settled, he took his own seat and gave a little cough, straightening the papers in front of him.

'You all know why you're here, so I won't waste time with preamble. This is the last will and testament of Mr Jago Tilley.' He gave a little cough. 'These are his bequests.'

Out of the corner of her eye, Loveday saw Billy Travis shift in his chair. His eyes were fixed on the papers.

'I'll start with the smaller bequests

first.' He proceeded to list various collections of ornaments that Jago had wanted Priddy to have. The old lady balled her hand into a fist and put it to her mouth. Loveday touched her arm and smiled at her. She doubted that any of the items would have any commercial value, but they obviously meant a lot to Priddy.

The solicitor was speaking again. Jago had left £1,000 to Billy. Judging by the disbelieving way the man was staring at the solicitor, he had been expecting more than this.

Loveday took a moment to study him critically. If what she had been told was right, Billy Travis was the barely-tolerated, greedy relative of Jago's. Priddy had told her that he'd crewed on the old man's fishing boat at one time, but there had never been any love lost between the two of them.

Loveday's eyes travelled over the cheap navy jacket and not-too-clean-looking white tee shirt. Travis's blue jeans were frayed at the knees, and he wore grubby grey trainers. She reminded herself that this was the man Sam had questioned about Jago's murder. She watched him look round and scowl at the others, and then back to the solicitor.

'Look, mate. I haven't got all day. Can we just get to the main business?'

The solicitor tried to conceal a frown.

'I was just about to do that, Mr Travis.'

They all waited. For a second there was silence in the room, then Rodney Timms cleared his throat again.

'The bulk of the estate — i.e., Mr Tilley's cottage in Marazion, and the rest of the contents not previously mentioned, that are still in the property today — he has bequeathed to . . . ' He paused; whether for dramatic effect or otherwise, Loveday wasn't sure. ' . . . to the Newlyn Fishermen's Federation, represented here today by Mr Penrose.'

Billy was on his feet, the veins in his neck standing out. Loveday thought he was going to haul the solicitor over the desk and smash his fist into his face. Ray Penrose must have thought so too, for he sprung up and grabbed the smaller man in an armlock.

Loveday glanced at Priddy and thought

she saw the woman's mouth quirk into a smile.

Billy was raging. He struggled free and faced up to the fisherman.

'There's no way Jago's left his place to you lot.' He turned and jabbed a finger at the solicitor, who loosened the knot in his tie and eased himself back in his chair.

'You've got this wrong!' Billy yelled.

'Sit down, please, Mr Travis. I haven't finished yet.'

He opened a drawer, lifted out a long white envelope and slid it across to Priddy.

'This is for you, Mrs Rodda.'

Priddy frowned.

'What is it?'

Rodney Timms shrugged.

'All I can tell you is that Mr Tilley came into my office three weeks ago, and wrote and sealed this letter with the instructions that it was to be handed over after his death.'

Billy now turned his venom on Priddy.

'Why has she got a letter and not me? What's going on here?'

Priddy folded the letter neatly and put

it into her handbag.

Billy exploded.

'Well, aren't you going to read it
. . . tell us what's in it?'

Priddy raised her blue eyes and gave
him an innocent stare.

'It was my name on the envelope, Billy,
so what's in it is private.'

Loveday turned to hide a smile as Billy
wheeled back round to vent his fury on
the solicitor.

'Is that it?' he barked. 'Is that all there
is?' He made a grab for the papers, but
Mr Timms got there before him and
swiped them away.

'I think you need to calm down, Mr
Travis.' There was a warning in the man's
voice.

Billy glared at him and then spun on
his heel, pushing past the big fisherman
as he slammed out of the room.

Priddy let out a long sigh and smiled.

'I wouldn't have missed this for the
world.' She raised her eyes to the ceiling.
'Nice one, Jago.'

They all left, turning down the
solicitor's offer of tea. Ray Penrose shook

Priddy's hand again outside and told her he would keep in touch with her. They watched his jaunty stride as he headed back up into the town. Loveday suspected the old lady had just wanted to get out of the office so she could get home and read Jago's letter in private; but as they walked down the hill towards her car, Loveday felt her arm being seized, and she was pulled into the direction of the Admiral Benbow pub.

'I feel a celebration sherry is called for.' Priddy smiled up into Loveday's surprised face. 'My treat.'

Priddy found a seat in one of the dark cushioned alcoves and waited until Loveday had returned with their drinks before snapping open her handbag.

'I can't wait any longer to read this. Do you mind, Loveday?'

Loveday shook her head, and lowered her voice.

'Would you like me to step outside for a minute to give you some privacy?'

Priddy smiled. 'Of course not. I'm sure you're just as curious as me to know what's in here.'

She slid out the letter and carefully eased it open, taking care not to tear it. With slightly trembling fingers, she unfolded the contents.

Loveday watched as the blue eyes moved along the rows of untidy writing. And then Priddy gasped, a hand at her throat.

'It's not bad news, is it?' Loveday said.

'No, it's not that,' Priddy said quietly. 'Jago has left me his mother's picture.'

Loveday blinked. Had she heard that right . . . his mother's picture?

'I don't understand,' she said. 'Is it valuable?'

'It was to Jago. That picture meant the world to him, and now he's given it to me.'

Loveday's mind reeled back to the missing picture Sam had asked her about. Was this what all the fuss was about? She frowned.

'I'm assuming this is the picture that went missing from Jago's cottage?'

Priddy nodded.

'Does the letter say where it is now?'

Priddy lifted her glass and downed the

last dregs of her sweet sherry. Her cheeks were already glowing pink.

'It's in my shed.' She tapped the letter. 'Jago says here that Billy was after it, so he hid it in my shed.'

Loveday let out an incredulous laugh.

'This just gets crazier and crazier.'

10

It was dark as they drove into Marazion, and Loveday's curiosity about the missing picture was growing by the minute. But surely a sketch of the dead man's mother would be of interest only to him? She could understand Priddy's delight, knowing Jago had entrusted into her safekeeping something that had been so special to him. She supposed it would be like having a part of him still around. But there was so much that didn't make sense.

Now that the burial had taken place, the police seemed to have relaxed their interest in the terrace. The incident van was still in place but the cordon of tape had gone, and Loveday was able to drive up to Priddy's cottage. They went inside and straight through to the kitchen to the back door, which Priddy unlocked. Glancing up at a row of hooks to her right, she asked Loveday to lift down a torch and the shed key, then the pair of them crept down the garden path like a couple of wary burglars.

The shed smelled peaty, which Loveday guessed probably came from the stack of well-used wooden seed boxes she could see in the beam of the torch. A rake, spade and hoe hung tidily from hooks. She shone the torch around the shed, stopping at a collection of plastic plant pots.

'What about down there? Can you see anything?'

Priddy rummaged and then straightened up, holding her back.

'There's something down there,' she said, not sure why they were whispering. 'You're more agile than me, my love. You have a look.'

Loveday handed over the torch and reached down, bringing out an old plastic supermarket bag that had been wedged into the corner. The whole thing seemed unlikely, but now that she was here she had to humour the old lady. The object inside the bag certainly did feel like a picture frame.

She handed the bag to Priddy, who clasped it to her chest and turned back to the cottage.

'Let's get back indoors. It's freezing out here,' she muttered, leading the way back to the warm kitchen.

Loveday relocked the shed and scurried after her. Priddy laid the bag carefully on the kitchen table and slid out the contents. It *was* a picture frame, which she held up for Loveday to see.

'There . . . ' She sounded triumphant. 'We've found it.'

Loveday eyed the picture. It was a sketch of a young woman. A shawl covered her head, the folds of the material falling in soft drapes around her shoulders. There was an ethereal innocence about the lovely young face that brought a lump to her throat. Loveday had been moved before by iconic works of art, but this was just a rough sketch, and yet it was wonderful.

Even with her untrained eye she could see it was well-drawn. She picked it up to examine it more closely, and her eyes fell on the signature. She blinked, and peered harder at the casual scrawl. It was faded, but could that be . . . ?

She pointed to it.

'Have you seen this, Priddy?'

The woman nodded.

'Walter Langley,' she said confidently. 'He was a painter in Newlyn when Jago's mother was a girl. She used to sit for him, and he would give her some of the sketches.'

Loveday stared at her. Her heart was beginning to pound. Walter Langley was the pioneer of the Newlyn School artists. His work was now revered and much-sought-after. She could only imagine what a previously-unknown sketch by him could be worth.

'Did Jago have more of these?' she said quietly.

'Just the five.' Priddy smiled affectionately at the picture. 'He kept them all together in this frame. He liked to rotate them every year on his mother's birthday. I think it was a kind of tribute to her.'

Loveday swallowed.

'Could you show me these other sketches?'

Priddy unclipped the frame and removed the wooden back while Loveday stared in disbelief as the rest of the sketches fluttered onto the table. Priddy counted them.

'All present and correct,' she said, smiling. 'I was worried that Billy might have got his hands on one or two of them, but they're all here.'

Loveday examined each one in turn. There were two more showing the same girl in different poses on Newlyn Beach. In both sketches she had a large wicker fish basket strapped to her back. Another showed the girl sitting on crumbling stone steps, with the harbour wall in the background. Loveday lifted the final sheet. It wasn't a sketch at all. It was a watercolour, and this time the girl had a baby in her arms.

Loveday pointed to the child.

'Is this Jago?'

'No, it's his mother's baby sister . . . Jago's aunt. Billy's mother.'

Loveday put her hands on top of her head. She could hardly believe what was in front of her. *Five* previously undiscovered works by Walter Langley — and one of them a watercolour. She wondered what the art world would make of this.

She forced herself to speak quietly, trying to control her growing excitement.

'Do you know who Walter Langley was, Priddy?'

Priddy turned her innocent blue eyes on Loveday.

'I told you. He was an artist, and quite a good one judging by these.'

Loveday slid out a chair and sat down. Were these sketches and the watercolour the reason Jago had been killed? Were these what his murderer had wanted? She had to tell Sam about this.

She glanced up at Priddy, who was now staring at the pictures with a look of horror. It was as though she had been reading Loveday's mind.

'Are you saying that these pictures are valuable?'

Loveday nodded slowly.

'They will all have to be verified as authentic, of course; but, yes, I think they could be very valuable.'

Priddy's voice shook.

'Is this why Jago was killed?' She waved a hand over the sketches spread around the table, her eyes wide with shock. 'Did he die for these?'

Loveday saw the spark of tears and went quickly round the table to put a comforting arm around the woman's shoulders.

'We don't know that. You're probably upsetting yourself for nothing.' But she could see that Priddy wasn't convinced.

'It all makes sense now. That's why he took down the pictures and hid them in my shed. Jago knew Billy was after them.' She gave a sudden gasp, staring wide-eyed at Loveday. 'It was *him*, wasn't it? It was Billy that killed Jago.'

The colour had drained from the old lady's face.

'I don't know, Priddy,' Loveday said gently. 'But I do think we have to tell the police about this.'

She checked her watch. It was almost 5.30. Sam would probably still be at the station. Except that he wasn't, so she left a message, asking him to call her. She tried his mobile number. It was unobtainable. She sighed. Cornwall being Cornwall, there were many places where mobile phone connections were unpredictable. She was thinking fast. The instrument was still in her hand.

'Would you mind if I took some pictures of these?' she asked.

Priddy shrugged.

'If you think it would help, but I don't see how. What about the police?'

'I'll keep trying,' Loveday said, using her phone to take a couple of shots of each of the images in turn. 'But in the meantime, I think we should put these away somewhere safe.'

Priddy shuddered.

'If Jago was killed for these pictures, then I don't want them anywhere near my cottage.'

Loveday watched her gather up the sketches and clip them back into the frame. She looked up.

'Can you take them, Loveday?'

'Well . . . of course . . . if that's what you want.'

'Please, Loveday,' she pleaded. 'At least until the police can sort this out.'

The woman looked so worried that Loveday was reluctant to leave her alone.

'Look, why don't you come back with me tonight? You've had an upsetting day and you shouldn't be here on your own.'

But Priddy waved the offer aside.

'Jane was after me spending a couple of nights with them. I'll give her a ring and tell her she can collect me after all.'

'Are you sure?'

Priddy nodded, and rose to get the notebook and pen she kept by her phone. She jotted down her daughter's phone number and address, and handed it over.

'This is where I'll be if the police want to get in touch.'

Loveday tucked the note into her pocket and slipped the wooden picture frame back into its plastic supermarket bag. She gave it a pat.

'I'll keep this safe for you.'

Sam still hadn't returned her call, so Loveday tried his mobile again before driving off. Still no answer.

She didn't notice the small red car parked just out of sight at the top of the terrace, or see the driver sliding it into gear and moving slowly after her.

Loveday's head was buzzing as she turned into her drive. She had the feeling that something monumental was about to happen, and she was right there in the middle of it.

When she got into her kitchen, she put the sketches on the table and reached for her phone to call Sam again when there was a knock on the back door.

'Come on in, Cassie,' she called.

Her friend hadn't yet changed into the familiar faded blue smock Loveday was used to seeing her in at home. She was still wearing her smart grey trouser-suit with its cream silk blouse. She pulled out a chair and sat down.

'So, how did it go at the solicitor's?'

So much seemed to have happened since then that Loveday hardly knew where to start. So she started at the beginning, finishing with the revelation about the Walter Langley sketches.

Cassie sank back in her chair.

'Wow! You don't do things by halves do you, Loveday? What does Sam have to say about all this?'

'I don't know. I haven't been able to reach him.' Then she had an idea. 'I think I might drive over to his place.' She nodded towards the sketches. 'This isn't something that should be explained over the phone.'

Cassie looked doubtful.

'Are you sure it's a good idea just to

turn up his house? What if he's
. . . entertaining a lady?'

Loveday narrowed her eyes at her
friend.

'I'm just saying . . . ' Cassie reasoned.
'You two aren't supposed to be together
any more . . . remember?'

Loveday did remember, but things were
different now. She just wasn't in the
mood to explain it to Cassie. She said,
'I'll try ringing him again before I leave
. . . but I am going.'

Cassie held up her hands.

'You know best, Loveday.'

Loveday's eyes fell on the sketches. She
didn't fancy driving about the countryside
with them in the back of her car. And she
wasn't happy about leaving them in her
cottage unattended. She picked up the
bag.

'Could I beg a huge favour, Cassie?
Could you keep an eye on these at your
house until I get back?'

Cassie's nose wrinkled.

'Are they very valuable?'

'They could be.'

Cassie sighed.

'Well, all right, but only until you can get Sam to take charge of them.'

Sam's house was in darkness as Loveday pulled up across the road from his gate. The driveway, where she knew he normally parked his car, was empty. She'd been here just twice before, and those times had been in the summer, when it was light. Even then, she'd felt there was a loneliness about the place. And the fact that his cottage was the end one in a terrace of three stone dwellings didn't appear to lessen that feeling.

It wasn't the kind of place she'd expected a single man to choose, but then Sam hadn't been single when he'd moved in. He'd been married to Tessa, his beautiful second wife, who had died at the hands of a drunk driver. The fact that Loveday was convinced Sam had never truly got over this was just another one of the reasons for their recent split.

She sat staring miserably up the empty drive, wishing she hadn't come now. She could just make out the little shed at the end that he'd told her Tessa had used as a workshop for her jewellery business. Sam had never been able to bring himself to get rid of all the equipment.

Loveday had been about to switch on the ignition and drive away when she saw the beam of Sam's car lights come over the brow of the hill, and his curious frown as he passed her and turned into his drive. She got out and strolled over.

'You should try picking up your messages sometimes,' she said.

He gave her a sheepish grin.

'Sorry. I've been out of the station most of the day and my personal mobile has lost its charge. What's up?'

'Can we do this inside? It's freezing out here.'

Sam reached into his car and Loveday caught a faint whiff of vinegar.

'Fish and chips,' he said, holding out the takeaway bag. 'I'll share with you.'

They went inside and he disappeared into the kitchen for plates and cutlery while Loveday plonked herself down on one of the two small sofas in the front room. The place was badly in need of decoration. Dark stained beams, that almost certainly weren't real, ran the full length of the ceiling, and the chimney-breast was encased in some kind of reconstituted stone. An electric fire sat in the open hearth, and Loveday went across to switch it on.

'Okay. What was so important that it brought you all the way out here?' Sam said, returning with a tray bearing two plates of delicious-smelling fish and chips.

'I think I've found your missing picture.' She stuffed a chip into her mouth and groaned with delight. Breakfast toast had been her last meal.

Sam was staring at her.

'Well, go on. Don't stop there.'

She recounted the afternoon's events, ending with the Walter Langley sketches now being in Cassie's care.

'I don't believe this. You mean that picture was in Priddy's shed all the time?' He had abandoned his takeaway and was reaching for his phone. 'I'll get someone to pick up those sketches.'

Loveday frowned.

'I thought your phone was dead?'

'Not this one . . . but you don't have this number.'

She heard him give DS Will Tregellis Cassie's address as she popped the last chip in her mouth and sank back on the sofa.

'So what happens now?'

Sam handed her a can of lager, apologizing that he had no wine.

'I shouldn't be telling you this, so it has to be in strictest confidence.'

Loveday nodded, tugging at the ring pull and raised the can to her lips.

'Malcolm and I visited an art dealer in St Ives that Billy Travis has been involved with in the past. We knew something was going on, but we had no idea what. If these sketches really are Langley's then it would explain a lot.'

Loveday was watching Sam's face. She could almost see his mind working.

She took a breath. 'Did Billy kill Jago for the sketches?'

Sam narrowed his eyes. 'I don't think so.'

'Well, it has to be this art dealer person,' she said.

'Not necessarily. If Paxton-Quinn — that's the art dealer — has told someone else about the sketches, then . . . ' He shook his head. All these ifs and buts were just so much speculation. They didn't actually know anything.

'We know that Jago Tilley is dead, and that somebody killed him,' said Loveday, reading his mind. 'And we know that Billy Travis knew about the sketches, and possibly passed on that information to this Mr Quinn, who possibly passed it on to a third person.'

Sam sighed. 'What we don't know is if these sketches are genuine. Anybody can sign their name to a picture. I'm no art expert, so I wouldn't know.'

'No, me neither,' said Loveday thoughtfully. 'But I know a lady who will. I'm seeing her tomorrow, actually. If I could take the sketches with me . . .'

Sam shook his head.

'Nice try, Loveday. But the sketches are going nowhere, not before I let forensics loose on them.'

It was more than an hour before Sam's mobile rang. Loveday snuggled into his back as he reached across to his bedside table. It was Will.

'It's Miss Ross's cottage, boss. You'd

better get down here.'

There were three police vehicles in the drive and lights blazed from all the downstairs rooms in Cassie and Adam's house. Loveday jumped out of Sam's car and raced to Cassie's back door. Her friend opened it and Loveday threw her arms around her.

'My God, Cassie. Are you all okay?'

Adam came through the kitchen and put a hand on his wife's shoulder.

'We're all fine.' He grimaced and nodded towards Loveday's cottage. 'Your place has taken a bit of knock. I can't believe we didn't hear them breaking in.'

Loveday flapped a hand.

'I'm not bothered about that. It's all just stuff. It's you and Cassie and the children I care about.' She bit her lip. 'This is all my fault, I should never have got you involved. I had no right asking you to look after those sketches.'

Cassie took Loveday's arm and walked her through to the sitting-room.

'You sit down; you look more shattered than any of us. Now if you promise to stay calm, I'll tell you all about it while

Adam gets us all a drink.' She sighed. 'Although there isn't that much to tell. The first we knew anything was wrong was when that Detective Sergeant Tregellis knocked on our door. He'd come to pick up the sketches, and then noticed that your back door had been forced. After that all hell just seemed to break loose.'

Adam returned with two large glasses of white wine and handed one to each of them. Loveday took a sip, relaxing as the icy liquid slid down her throat.

'Did the police catch anyone?'

Cassie shrugged.

'I've no idea.'

It was half an hour before Sam appeared. Adam drew him into the room.

'You look all in,' he said. 'Can I get you a drink?'

Loveday jumped up and ran to him, wrapping her arms around him. Out of the corner of her eye she saw Cassie smile at Adam.

'Better not, but thanks for the offer,' Sam said, tilting up Loveday's chin, so that he could look into her face.

'They've made a bit of a mess of your

cottage, I'm afraid. It's nothing structural, just drawers turned out, cupboards emptied and their contents strewn about the place.' His mouth stretched into a hard line. 'And I can't see any sign of your laptop.'

Loveday met his eyes.

'This was no coincidence, was it, Sam?'

Sam shook his head.

'I doubt it.'

'They were looking for the sketches, weren't they?' Loveday frowned. 'Which means they must have seen me leaving Priddy's place with them.' She banged the heel of her hand against her temple. 'Stupid . . . how could I have been so stupid? I made no attempt to hide the bag with the sketches, and they followed me.'

Sam's arms tightened around her. 'Don't be so hard on yourself, Loveday. There's no way you could have known. But you can't stay at the cottage tonight . . . '

'You know you're welcome here, Loveday,' Cassie interrupted.

'Or you could just come back home with me,' Sam said.

Loveday glanced at Cassie.

'I think I'd better stick around here for the moment, but thanks, Sam.'

'Are you sure?'

Loveday saw the concern in his eyes and glanced away to hide a sting of tears in her own. She nodded.

'Right, well I'm giving you my police mobile number. You can reach me on this . . . anytime.'

He tipped her chin up and kissed her softly on the mouth.

'Anytime . . . remember that.'

He released her gently, nodding his thanks to Cassie and Adam.

After he'd gone, Loveday returned to her chair, tucking her feet under her.

Cassie gave her a teasing smile.

'So when did all this happen?'

Loveday's cheeks pinked up.

'All what?'

'You know . . . you and Sam. I take it it's all back on again?'

'We're . . . discussing it,' Loveday said coyly, her colour deepening.

11

It was after midnight when Loveday heard the SOCO team's vehicles drive away. She was lying in bed in Cassie and Adam's spare room; staring into the darkness, imagining the chaos in her once-lovely cottage. There could be no doubt, the intruder was looking for the Langley sketches and watercolour. But how could they have known that she had them? Loveday shivered. She had definitely been followed!

She sat up in bed, her mind flashing back over the previous day's events. Only those present at the reading of the will could have known about those sketches. But wait — how was even that possible when the actual sketches were never mentioned? The information about their whereabouts was in the private, sealed letter that Jago had left for Priddy. Only she and Priddy had known they were in her shed.

Loveday swung her legs out of the bed and went across to the window. From here she had a much higher view of the bay, and the dark shape of the castle. She stared across the water to the lights of Penzance and Newlyn. Billy would have guessed what was in that letter. Had he followed them home and waited in the shadows outside Priddy's cottage to see Loveday leave with the bag of sketches? He'd left the solicitor's office before anyone else. Could he have met someone outside and passed on the information, and could this third person be the one who had followed them?

Her head was reeling. The very idea that someone had been lying in wait, watching for Loveday to leave Priddy's cottage, sent a shiver down her spine. If she hadn't been carrying the sketches, would it have been the old lady's cottage that got ransacked? That would have been so much worse. Whoever had killed Jago was certainly ruthless enough to try again. Sam had insisted on a uniformed officer being posted outside Priddy's door all night. At least the old lady's home and her belongings would be safe.

Loveday didn't remember getting back into bed and falling into a fitful sleep, but she must have because she woke with a start when Cassie tapped on the door and appeared in a long blue dressing-gown.

Loveday squinted at the clock. It was 7.30, and still dark outside.

Cassie put the cup and saucer down on the bedside table and gave her a concerned look.

'How are you feeling this morning?'

Loveday struggled up to a sitting position and rubbed her eyes, glancing at the tea. 'Thanks, Cassie. You're a lifesaver.' She reached for the cup. 'And I'm fine. It's your poor cottage that I'm worried about.'

'Well there's no need. The insurance will pay for any damage, and you'll be pleased to learn that all your stuff is also covered. Adam checked our policy.'

Loveday hadn't even considered how much property she might have lost. Sam had said her laptop was missing.

'I need to get over there and check it all out myself,' she said, finishing her tea.

'I'll come with you.' Cassie was already heading for the door. 'Give me ten minutes to wash and dress and I'll see you downstairs.'

The grey dawn light was creeping across the sky when they opened the back door of the cottage and went in. Loveday's eyes scanned the chaotic mess in the kitchen with growing dismay. Cupboard doors lay open, their contents strewn about the room. It was as though someone had swept an arm over the shelves, hurling everything to the floor. Even the fridge had been ransacked.

The sitting-room was worse. Cushions had been upturned from the chairs, rugs pulled up, and Loveday's books, which she had so lovingly displayed on the shelves, had been scattered in untidy, irreverent heaps about the room. The drawers in the small desk where her laptop had sat had been wrenched open. Her camera, and other photographic equipment, was also missing.

Loveday swallowed, hardly daring to venture into the bedroom. It looked like a jumble sale. Clothes from her wardrobe had been pulled out and tossed in all directions, and the drawers in the chest and dressing-table had been emptied onto the floor. The duvet, sheets and pillows had been hauled off the bed and thrown in a heap on top of her clothes.

Loveday bit her lip, but was unable to stop the hot tears rolling down her cheeks.

'Oh, Loveday,' Cassie said, coming to put an arm round her shoulders. 'I'm so sorry. This is terrible.'

The tremble in her friend's voice just made her feel worse.

'I feel so violated, Cassie,' she said shakily. 'I can't bear to think someone was in here, touching my things, abusing my possessions like this.'

Her eye caught the spill of photographs on the rug in front of the fire. It was the set of proofs she had brought back from Mylor's photoshoot with Sabine De Fries. She quickly gathered them up, slipped them back into the large brown envelope that was only slightly torn, and cast another anguished glance around the room.

'At least they didn't find what they were looking for.'

Cassie cleared her throat. The businesswoman was taking over. 'Okay, now that we know what needs doing, let's go back to the house. I think Adam's cooking some breakfast,' she said. 'We'll both feel better with some strong coffee and some food inside us.'

Food was the last thing Loveday wanted; but she said nothing and followed Cassie back to her kitchen, where Sophie and Leo were already tucking into bowls of cereal. Adam was whisking eggs, and had one eye on the toaster. He glanced up, and Loveday saw the look of concern he shot his wife, but he covered it with an immediate smile.

'Would scrambled eggs on toast suit you two?'

'Great, thanks.' Loveday smiled back.

She'd dropped her mobile phone into her pocket earlier and now it had begun to trill. She fished it out and clicked the answer button.

'Merrick!'

'Sam's just been on. He told me what

happened at your place last night. God, Loveday, are you all right?'

She stifled a sigh. This was going to be a day of people asking if she was 'all right'.

'Of course I am, but thanks for asking.'

'Did they take much?'

'My laptop and camera stuff. The rest is mostly mess.' She glanced up at Cassie, who gave her a reassuring smile. 'I might be a bit late getting in today, though.'

Merrick let out an exasperated sigh. They didn't work every Saturday, but they were way behind schedule this month, and everyone had agreed to treat this as a normal working day.

'What are you talking about? You don't imagine I'm expecting you to come into the office today? You stay where you are, Loveday. Sounds to me like you have plenty to do there.'

'But . . . ' Loveday was remembering her full diary, including that interview later with Rebecca Monteith at the Penzance gallery.

'No buts,' Merrick cut in. 'Keri and I will sort things out here.'

'Are you sure?' she asked uncertainly.

'Perfectly sure. You just let Cassie and Adam take care of you.'

'Thanks, Merrick.' She smiled at the phone, thinking Merrick was sounding much more like his old self, and wondered if he had sorted out the legal thing with Cadan.

Cassie looked up as Loveday clicked off the connection.

'Everything all right?'

Loveday nodded.

'It was Merrick, telling me not to go into the office today.'

'Quite right, too,' Adam said, spooning the eggs onto slices of brown toast.

She was about to tell him not to dish up too much for her, but the eggs did smell appetizing. And when she sat down to eat, she realized that she was hungry after all.

When her offer to help wash up was turned down, Loveday picked up her phone to call Sam, but he beat her to it.

'I would have rung sooner, but I thought you deserved a lie-in this morning.' He was sounding surprisingly chirpy, and Loveday wondered if it had anything to do with the fact that they were now a couple again. The memory gave her a warm glow. She smiled into the phone.

'And before you ask . . . I'm fine.' She told him about Merrick's call and his insistence on her not turning up at the office. 'Was that your doing, Sam?'

'Well, hardly. Merrick's not going to listen to me.' But she knew that he had, and she was grateful.

'Cassie is going to help me sort out the cottage,' she said.

He tut-tutted at the other end, and said, 'You're amazing, Loveday. Does nothing faze you?'

She was glad he hadn't witnessed her teary reaction earlier when she'd stood in the cottage surveying the chaos. She thought about inviting him to join her at the Penzance gallery, for she was still determined to go. She had asked Cassie to print out the pictures of the Walter Langley sketches that she'd taken on her mobile phone, and was planning to show them to Rebecca Monteith. She knew

Sam would be interested in some knowledgeable feedback about the artwork, but he was bound to frown on her continued involvement in the case.

'Leave some of that tidying-up for me,' Sam said, as their call came to an end. 'I'll be over this evening.'

There was a moment's silence and she knew he was waiting for her approval of the suggestion.

'I'll look forward to that, Sam,' she said quietly.

Loveday was feeling distinctly more cheerful about her situation as she and Cassie headed back to the cottage. They had begun to put the kitchen straight when they heard the footsteps outside. Both assuming it was Adam, neither of them had turned to look out the window. There was a quick knock, and then the kitchen door opened, and Priddy's distressed blue eyes went from one to the other.

'I've just got back from Jane's. It's all round the village about your poor cottage, Loveday.' Her incredulous gaze scanned the room, and she clamped her hands to her face. 'Oh my goodness. This is all my fault. If I hadn't got you involved in my business, Loveday, none of this would have happened.'

'Of course it's not your fault, Priddy,' Loveday said, reaching to upright an upturned chair and nodding the old lady into it. 'The fault is all mine. I should have been more careful.'

She glanced round the kitchen, wondering if she could find some teabags, but Priddy was rapidly getting over her initial shock. She stood up, slipped off her coat and hung it from a hook on the back of the door. Rolling up her sleeves, she said, 'Right. Where would you two like me to start?'

Loveday and Cassie exchanged amused glances, but Priddy insisted, holding out her plump hard-working hands.

'I didn't get these callouses from sitting by the fire with my feet up. Just tell me what to do.'

Cassie shrugged.

'Well, if you're sure you want to help . . . ' Cassie waved a hand around the kitchen. 'You could help us to pick up all this cutlery. We need to wash it and put it back in the drawer.'

'I can do that,' she said.

By mid-morning the kitchen looked back to normal, and Cassie and Priddy had a made a start in the sitting-room while Loveday tackled the bedroom. She straightened as she picked the last garment from the floor, pushing a strand of dark hair out of her eyes and tucking it behind her ear.

'I can't believe how hard you two have worked. I thought it would take a week to sort this lot out.'

Priddy flashed her a twinkling smile.

'Many hands make light work, that's what my old mother always said, and she was right.'

'She certainly was,' Cassie said, draping her arms over the shoulders of the other two. 'I think this calls for three lovely cups of tea.'

★   ★   ★

It was just after lunchtime when Loveday arrived at the Penzance gallery. She'd visited it before, and had been fascinated by the story of the Newlyn artists. She knew that Walter Langley had been the first to settle in Newlyn in 1882, and that he'd founded the colony of artists that was now known as the Newlyn School. She'd also discovered that he'd been born in Birmingham, and had lived and painted for a time in Brittany before discovering Cornwall.

It came as second nature to research the person she was going to interview. She needed to know as much as she could about her new subject. Loveday knew she wouldn't necessarily use all the information she'd collected, but the more she had at her fingertips, the more depth her article would have.

She followed the directions given to her by the receptionist, and tracked Rebecca down to a small room off one of the upper-floor galleries. She was behind a table covered in sketches and charts. Ledgers and writing tools were assembled on a table behind her. It looked more like a graphic design studio than the workplace of an art historian.

Rebecca lowered a pair of huge, black-rimmed spectacles and smiled. 'Ah, you've found me. Not many people know about my little garret up here.'

Loveday returned her smile.

'You can blame the friendly reception-ist downstairs.'

The woman got up and came round to shake Loveday's hand.

'Sorry about the other day. The cathedral gift shop can get a bit hectic, particularly at this time of year. I shouldn't have suggested it as a meeting place.'

'No problem,' Loveday said. 'But this was a much better idea because now I can see you in your own environment. If it's all right with you, I'd like to take some pictures. Perhaps we can have a stroll around the gallery?' Taking pictures on her mobile phone might not be as effective as the ones produced by her expensive camera, but they would serve the purpose. At the end of the day, Mylor would be responsible for the main photoshoot.

Loveday was keen to get her interview done and dusted before she mentioned Priddy's Walter Langley sketches.

211

Rebecca led the way through various rooms, where works by Cornish artists were tastefully displayed. They paused before an enormous watercolour of distraught women weeping by the quayside of a Cornish fishing village.

'It's the aftermath of a disaster at sea,' Rebecca explained. 'The women are waiting for news of whose husbands have survived and whose have perished.'

Loveday had seen and been moved by this particular Walter Langley painting before. She glanced at the title: *Among the Missing — Scene in a Cornish Fishing Village, 1884.*

'The museum doesn't sell any prints of this work,' Rebecca explained. 'It's considered to be too sad.'

Loveday nodded. 'I can see what you mean.'

The gallery had been filling up as they walked around, and Loveday was pleased to see so many young families here.

When they got back to Rebecca's office, she produced a flask of coffee and two mugs.

'I've enjoyed our little chat. Will you

have enough information for your article?'

'More than enough, I should think,' Loveday said, reaching into her bag. She pulled out the printed copies of the snaps she'd taken of Priddy's sketches.

'I wonder if I could ask your opinion on these?'

She spread the images out on the table.

Rebecca put the flask of coffee aside and stared at them.

'What are these?' She picked up each one separately and examined it. 'Where did you get them?'

Loveday explained about Priddy's bequest to an increasingly astounded Rebecca.

'And you have the originals of these?'

Loveday frowned.

'Not exactly. The police have them, but they belong to the lady I mentioned. They're sketches that Walter Langley made of Jago Tilley's mother when she was a girl. Apparently, she lived next door to him in Newlyn, and frequently used to pose for him.' She glanced up at the woman. 'Don't you think they are evocative of that whole Newlyn School thing? I mean, it must have been an amazing time when artists,

213

like Stanhope Forbes and his wife Elizabeth, and all the others, lived and painted right here.'

Rebecca smiled.

'Don't forget the Lamorna group . . . Alfred Munnings, Dame Laura Knight, Lamorna Birch . . . I'm sure they could all tell a tale or two if they were still with us.'

She glanced down at Loveday's printed sketches again, tracing her finger over the face of the young woman who had been drawn with a shawl covering her head. 'I would have to see the originals of course before I could make any real assessment, but these certainly look like Langley's work . . . and this one is very much like a painting he called *Newlyn Fishergirl*.'

Loveday's eyes lit up.

'Is it here in the gallery?'

Rebecca shook her head.

'Sadly, no. It's in a private collection, although it has been exhibited here. I'm sure we could find pictures of it on the Internet.'

Loveday ran the tip of her tongue over lips to moisten them before she spoke

again. 'If these sketches are authentic . . . ' She hesitated. 'What might they
be worth?'

Rebecca's chair creaked as she leaned
back and rolled her eyes to the ceiling.

'Undiscovered Langley sketches . . . ?
Tens of thousands of pounds, I should
think . . . maybe more. It would depend
on who wanted to buy them.'

'Would the museum buy them?'

'The museum doesn't have unlimited
funds,' Rebecca said. 'Practically all the
works you see here have been purchased
through substantial public and private
donations.' She smiled. 'But we are getting
ahead of ourselves. Why are the sketches
being held by the police?'

Loveday looked away, not sure how
much she should say. She decided to be
cautious. The last thing she wanted was to
incur Sam's wrath again . . . not now that
they were getting on so well; and, besides,
she'd found out what she wanted to
know. The sketches were valuable — but
were they worth enough to warrant killing
someone for them?

12

Loveday had one more quick call to make before driving back to Marazion. She had promised Sabine that she would drop in with the proofs of the photoshoot. They were of inferior quality to how the finished prints would look, but at least they would give her an idea of what the end result could look like.

She'd expected Falmouth to be busy this close to Christmas, and she hadn't been wrong. The narrow streets were crammed with shoppers who spilled onto the road when the pavements got too crowded, reducing Loveday's progress along Market Street to a crawl.

Sabine's shop was halfway along and she glanced into the seductively festive window display as she drove past. The boutique owner had introduced a new line in sexy lingerie to her Christmas stock and she seemed to be doing brisk business. Further along the street Loveday turned left and drove down the steep slope into the waterfront car park. She had to make two circuits of it before she found a space. Checking her purse for change, she went in search of a pay machine. She was on the way back to her car when she spotted a familiar vehicle. It was Cadan's small white sports car. In the murky half-light of late afternoon he hadn't seen her. What was he doing in Falmouth?

Moving swiftly through the ranks of stationary vehicles, she tried to keep track of where he had pulled in, but so many cars were coming and going that it was impossible. She put her ticket on the dashboard of the Clio, and picked up her brown leather shoulder bag and the pack of prints from the passenger seat. Just as she closed the door she spotted Cadan striding across the car park. She watched him get a ticket from the same machine she had used; this time, determined not to lose him, she kept her eyes glued on the moving figure. He had found a space just a few bays along.

She thought about hurrying after him to say hello, but there was something about his body language that made her hold back. He could have been in town for some last-minute shopping before the stores closed, but she didn't think so. She doubted if Christmas shopping came anywhere on Cadan Tremayne's list of priorities. He'd probably never bought a gift for anyone in his life.

He lost no time in throwing his ticket onto the dashboard of his car and heading up the slope to join the shoppers in busy Market Street.

It was properly dark now, and the faces of the shoppers, laden with their brightly-coloured bags and parcels, were beginning to show signs of weariness. After a day of this, most of them probably just wanted to get home, Loveday thought. Cadan was only a few yards in front of her now, dipping in and out of the crowds. She wondered if he'd come to Falmouth to meet someone. The Bunch of Grapes at the top of the hill was the most likely pub for a meeting, but he strode past the place without even giving it a glance.

Loveday had no idea why she was following him. It was completely none of

218

her business, except that his presence in Cornwall was causing his older brother, Merrick, a lot of grief. And Loveday didn't like her friends being treated that way.

He was moving quickly and it was all she could do to keep up with him. This was obviously not a shopping trip for he showed no interest in the shop windows glittering with Christmas lights and tinsel. She glanced at her watch. It was five o'clock. They were nearing the boutique now. If she kept up this ridiculous pursuit, Sabine's shop would be closed and her trip to Falmouth would have been wasted. She sighed. The purpose of Cadan's visit would have to remain a mystery.

But as she slowed her pace she realized that he was no longer in sight. She had allowed her concentration to slip and now she had lost him. She shook her head — deciding, as she paused in front of the boutique window, that she would have made a rubbish spy.

Sabine's pink-and-black window display was not to Loveday's taste, but then she wasn't here to purchase anything. And, judging by how brisk business was looking inside the boutique, Sabine didn't need her custom anyway.

And then she caught her breath, her heart beginning to race. Even from the back, Cadan's large frame, in his expensive-looking camel coat, was unmistakable. What was he doing here in Sabine's boutique?

Her thoughts leapt ahead. He could be buying some sexy underwear for a lady friend. What would be odd about that? But why here, at this little shop in Falmouth, when he had the all the excellent Truro stores on his doorstep?

It had come on to sleet and shoppers were now hurrying past, clutching parcels and tugging up collars against the biting December wind as they made their ways to the bus queues and car parks.

The icy drops falling on the glass were causing the boutique's window to steam up, but Loveday could still see inside to where Sabine was serving a customer. She looked up and saw Cadan, and for a second Loveday thought she detected a flash of annoyance in the cool green stare. Then Sabine slid her eyes to the left, indicating the door behind the counter. Cadan glanced briefly around him, then moved swiftly around the counter and through the door that led into the back shop — and Sabine's apartment.

Loveday blinked, trying to take in what she had just witnessed. So Cadan and Sabine knew each other? It had to be more than just a passing acquaintance for him to drive all the way to Falmouth on a wintery December afternoon.

She was remembering those gent's toiletries in the sumptuous bathroom upstairs. Was Cadan Sabine's mystery lover?

The sleet had now turned to flakes of snow and Loveday cursed as she brushed a hand over her wet hair. She was reluctant to go into the shop now. Something was going on here, and she was certain it was something that this woman wouldn't want her knowing about. Hugging the packet of pictures, she made her way back to the car park.

The snow was getting heavier and she

swiped at the thick flakes that clung to her lashes. Her mind was whirring, but there was no way she could think straight with the crowds pressing around her like this. She stepped up her pace, anxious to get back to the seclusion of the Clio.

Everyone seemed to be heading for home now, and a long line of vehicles was queuing to leave the car park. Loveday brushed the snow from her shoulders as she zapped the car door open and slid thankfully inside. She sat there for a few minutes, watching the other vehicles move slowly past, still trying to get her head round this new discovery about Cadan and Sabine.

Cassie had joked about the woman having a boyfriend with a weakness for gambling. At the time it had crossed Loveday's mind that Cadan Tremayne might be that man. It now looked as if she might have been right; and if he was, and Cassie's information was accurate, then it might also confirm something she had only vaguely suspected — that Merrick's brother had serious gambling debts.

She clicked in her seat belt and started

the engine, edging the Clio into the line of traffic. The entire car park seemed to be on the move. Driving back to Marazion in this heavy snow was going to take all of her concentration.

The trek out of town was painfully slow, with the traffic more often at a standstill than moving. It seemed to take forever to climb the hill and reach the main road. Even at full speed, the car's wipers were making hardly any impression on clearing the swirling snow from the windscreen. In the beam of her headlights she could see it collecting and lying on the verges. She just hoped she could reach Marazion before it got much worse.

The traffic on the main road had once again slowed to a crawl, and Loveday had to concentrate on the road signs she passed to make sure she was even on the right road. All she could do now was to keep a steady distance from the red tail-lights of the car in front. As long as she could see them she felt safe.

Her phone began to trill in her bag, and she cursed herself for not remembering to connect it up to the hands-free system before she set off. She hadn't told anyone where she was going. It was probably Sam. He'd be worrying about her.

She felt she had been driving for hours. Surely she must be close now to the first of the two roundabouts that would take her down to Marazion? But the snow was so disorientating that she wasn't certain. She peered into what had now become a blizzard. She couldn't afford to miss her turning. But it was another twenty minutes before the welcome sign came into view.

Loveday let out a sigh of relief as she carefully negotiated the roundabout, taking the first exit that put her on the hill down into Marazion. Carefully, she cruised down the curving road and into the centre, determined not to miss the familiar stone gateposts that flanked the drive to Cassie and Adam's house — and her cottage.

A wave of relief washed over Loveday when she saw Sam's car in the drive and her cottage all lit up. The back door was flung open as she pulled up, and Sam, his coat pulled over his head, sprinted out to help her from the car and rush her inside.

'Where have you been, Loveday?' he exploded. 'I've been out of my mind with worry.'

She slipped off her coat and hung it on the back of the door.

'Well you shouldn't have, because I was fine.' But she couldn't hide the fact that she was still shaking from her scary drive through the blizzard.

He gave her an exasperated frown and then put his arms around her.

'I really was worried about you,' he murmured into her hair. Then he tipped up her chin and she saw the concern in his dark brown eyes.

She reached up and kissed him.

'You're right. I should have told Cassie where I was going. I just wasn't expecting it to snow like this.' She gave him a teasing grin. 'Am I forgiven?'

He sighed and waggled a finger at her.

'Just don't do it again.'

There was a faint smell of cooking that made Loveday aware of the hollow emptiness in her stomach. She sniffed.

'It's a Chinese takeaway,' he said. 'We'll have to reheat it.'

He took her hand and led her into the sitting-room. The books that she had temporarily shoved onto the shelves had all been lovingly rearranged in their previous order, and a fire crackled in the grate. The lamps had been switched on and the room looked very cosy.

'There's wine chilling in the fridge.' He gave her a sideways glance. 'But I think a mug of hot chocolate might be more appropriate at the moment.'

Loveday sat down by the fire and smiled up at him. She wasn't about to argue with that. As he disappeared back into the kitchen she let her head sink back onto the cushions and closed her eyes, enjoying the warmth of the fire on her face. She didn't mind in the least being spoiled.

'It really was like a nightmare out there tonight, Sam,' she said when he returned with their hot drinks. 'I thought I'd never get home . . . and then to find you here . . . ' She gave him a coy smile and narrowed her eyes. 'How did you get in, anyway? I don't remember giving you your key back.'

'Blame Cassie,' he grinned.

Loveday closed her eyes again, feeling luxuriously safe.

'Remind me to thank her . . . in the morning.'

As they drank their hot chocolate, Loveday told Sam about Cadan's visit to Sabine De Fries's boutique.

He shrugged.

'So he has a girlfriend. What's unusual about that?'

Loveday sat forward, eyeing him earnestly.

'It's interesting because Cassie told me that Sabine had a boyfriend with gambling debts — and she was trying to raise funds to help him.'

Sam put his mug down on the coffee table.

'And you think that this boyfriend is Cadan?'

'Well, don't you?' Loveday said.

'I suppose he could be,' Sam said slowly. 'What I don't understand is what you were doing there in the first place.'

Loveday uncurled herself from her chair and went to find the envelope that contained the copies of Mylor Ennis's pictures.

She took them out and spread them on the low table.

'I wanted to show her these. They're for the article I'm planning for the spring edition.'

Sam picked up one of the pictures, studying it.

'This is Sabine De Fries?'

Loveday nodded.

'Don't tell me you know her?'

'Not exactly, but . . . '

He reached for his phone and punched in a number. Loveday stared at him.

'What is it, Sam? What's wrong?'

'Amanda?' he said when his call was answered. 'Can you run a check on a Sabine De Fries?' He repeated the details Loveday had just given him for the woman's boutique. 'And get back to me on this number as soon as you can.'

Loveday's eyes were wide with interest.

'What's going on, Sam?'

He tapped the picture.

'Probably nothing, but she looks a bit like the woman Malcolm and I saw at Zachariah Paxton-Quinn's gallery in St Ives.'

She stared at him.

'I told you about him. He's that glorified fence Billy Travis cuts deals with.' He glanced back to Sabine's picture and shook his head. 'I'm probably wrong. We didn't exactly get a good look at her — ' The trill of his mobile cut off the end of his sentence as he made a grab for the phone.

'Yes, Amanda?'

Loveday could only hear his side of the conversation, but it was obvious the police computer hadn't thrown up any information about Sabine.

'Of course, she might be using an alias,' Loveday said thoughtfully, when Sam had disconnected from his call.

His brows came down and he grinned at her.

'It's not the movies, Loveday. I don't think we're in the middle of a spy drama here.'

She clicked her tongue at him.

'You know what I mean. She could very easily be using the name Sabine De Fries for professional purposes. She has a bit of an accent and she told me she was from

Amsterdam. Actually, Cassie might know more. It was her who suggested doing the article on Sabine's boutique in the first place.' She uncurled herself from her chair. 'Shall I ask her?'

'Well, not right now . . . '

But Loveday was already on her way to the kitchen for her phone. Her voice drifted through.

'Cassie? What? Yes, I'm fine. I want to pick your brains.'

Sam listened, amused, as Loveday asked her friend if she knew Sabine's real name. There was silence for a few minutes as Cassie spoke, and then Loveday's voice again.

'Oh, would you, Cassie? I would really appreciate that. Sam and I will be here all night if you do find out anything.'

Sam hid a smile. So he wasn't to be sent out into the cold December night to find his way home. He hadn't been sure.

He got out of his chair and headed for the kitchen. 'I think it's time we ate,' he said.

It was two hours later when they heard Cassie tap at the back door. Loveday got up and went into the kitchen to let her in. She grinned at the sight of her friend in bright red wellie boots, standing in a pool of melting snow, brushing more of it from her coat and shaking out her hair.

'Oh my word,' Loveday exclaimed. 'Is it as bad as that out there?' She went to the window and looked out. It was still snowing heavily; not that she needed any more proof.

Sam rose from his chair as they came in.

'Can I get you a drink, Cassie?'

Cassie eyed their wineglasses.

'Is there any more of that?'

'I'm sure I can find some,' Sam said, heading for the fridge. He returned seconds later with a new bottle and a fresh glass for Cassie.

'Well?' Loveday asked excitedly, as Sam poured the wine. 'What have you found out?'

Cassie accepted a glass with a nod of thanks.

'I had to dig deep. Rachel put me on to Carol, who suggested I ring Deborah, who told me to try — '

'Okay,' Loveday laughed, putting up her hand. 'We get the picture, Cassie. Just tell us what you know.'

Cassie raised the glass to her lips and took a sip before flashing a conspiratorial glance from one to the other.

'Well, as far as any of them know, Sabine De Fries is her real name, and she *is* Dutch. She also owns a very swanky 28-foot motor cruiser in Falmouth Marina, which is how my people know her.'

'Wow!' said Loveday, sitting forward, her eyes intent on her friend's face. 'Anything else?'

Cassie frowned. 'What do you mean, *anything else*? Isn't that enough? I'm not a private eye, you know. I leave all that stuff to you two. Besides — ' She sat back and crossed her arms. ' — I thought I'd done rather well.'

'And so you did, Cassie,' Sam said, bestowing his most endearing smile on her, and sending a scowl in Loveday's direction. But it was lost on her, because Loveday was deep in thought.

And then she said, 'I still don't understand. If she's wealthy, why is she running that tiny little boutique in Falmouth? Judging by the style of that apartment she has over the shop, I would have thought running one of the big fashion houses in Paris or Rome would have been more her style.'

'The money comes from her family,' Sam said. 'Amanda looked her up. Sabine De Fries's parents, Frieda and Erik, own a string of boutique hotels all over Europe. They're rolling in it.'

'Sabine did tell me that,' Loveday cut in, 'but she gave the distinct impression that it was just a small operation.'

'If money is no object,' Cassie said, 'that's probably why she is bailing out this boyfriend — the one with the gambling problem.' She slipped her empty glass onto the table to join Loveday's, and stifled a yawn. 'It's getting past my bedtime, folks, so if there's not going to be any great scandal unfolding here, I might as well get off.'

Loveday followed Cassie to the back door and helped her to struggle back into her red wellies and coat.

'Thanks for going to all that trouble. I

really appreciate it.'

Cassie turned and narrowed her eyes suspiciously.

'Is there something you're not telling me, Loveday?'

'What ... no, of course not.' She wasn't ready to disclose her suspicion to Cassie that Sabine's gambling boyfriend could be her boss's brother.

'So you're still going ahead with Sabine's feature in the magazine?'

Loveday smiled. 'Well, that's the plan. I don't see any reason to change it.' Although she thought it would make a better story if the woman was prepared to tell her why she'd chosen to open a business in Falmouth when she apparently had the whole of Europe at her feet.

When Loveday returned to the fireside, she noticed that Sam had refilled their glasses, and was gazing into the flames.

'What's up?' she said, lifting her glass and curling up beside him on the sofa.

'Nothing,' Sam said, putting an arm around her. 'I'm fine.'

But Loveday could tell that he obviously wasn't. She guessed he was still brooding about Jack and Maddie and her heart went out to him. Her suggestion that they should come to Cornwall hadn't really been practical, not while this murder investigation was still ongoing.

She wriggled round to face him. 'I haven't told you where else I went today.'

Sam gave her a wary look. 'Why am I getting this sinking feeling in the pit of my stomach?'

Loveday put up her hands. 'Don't worry. I wasn't interfering in your police stuff. I was only doing my job.'

He frowned, waiting for her to go on.

'Merrick told me not to go into the office today . . . right?'

Sam nodded.

'But he didn't say not to proceed with the interview I had already set up.'

'Which was?'

'I told you, Rebecca Monteith, the art expert who's seconded to do some archive work at the Penzance gallery. She has a special interest in the Newlyn School.' She paused, looking up at him.

Sam was beginning to see where this was going.

'Well, naturally I asked her about the Langley sketches of Jago Tilley's mother.'

'Go on,' Sam said slowly.

Loveday took a breath. 'Rebecca thinks they could be quite valuable . . . worth thousands of pounds . . . maybe more.'

Sam looked at her from under his brows. 'An art expert said that without even seeing the sketches?'

'I showed her the pictures,' she said quickly. 'The ones I took with my phone in Priddy's kitchen. Cassie printed a set out for me.'

Sam shook his head, laughing.

'Your resourcefulness constantly amazes me, Loveday.'

'I'm good at my job, Sam,' she said, meeting his eyes. 'But we will obviously have to check the authenticity of the sketches before we consider anything else.

'However, if they *are* valuable, that would surely be a good motive for murdering poor old Jago, which puts that horrible nephew of his right back in the picture.' She grinned at him. 'No pun meant.'

'In the frame,' he corrected her, grinning. 'The phrase is *in the frame*. And

I think you're getting ahead of yourself again, Loveday. Leave the detective work to me.'

The mention of the picture reminded her of Edward Tremayne's stolen painting. She sat up.

'You didn't tell me Merrick's place had been burgled a few weeks ago.'

Sam shrugged. 'Merrick wanted it kept quiet.'

'Didn't you ever wonder why?'

'No, that's his business. Ours is to find that stolen painting, which we're still investigating. And, as you're well aware, Loveday, since it's an ongoing case, I can't discuss it with you.'

Loveday traced a finger around the rim of her glass. 'I know that, Sam. It's just that . . . well, I've been thinking.'

'Yes,' he said slowly, his eyebrow arching.

'Well, it might be an inside job. If Cadan owes money to that casino in Plymouth . . . ' She gave him an innocent stare. ' . . . well, it's not impossible that he stole the painting to raise the money to cover his gambling debts.'

Sam gave a disbelieving sigh. 'Like I said, Loveday — it's an ongoing investigation and I can't discuss it.'

'No, I understand that. It's just that I was thinking, if you were to go to Plymouth and interview the owner of that casino — in the line of duty, of course — it would give you the chance to catch up with Jack and Maddie before they go off to Florida.'

13

Long after Loveday had fallen asleep, Sam lay awake staring into the darkness.

He had considered that Cadan might be responsible for the theft of his father's painting. He had even routinely questioned him, but that had been more as a witness. There was no evidence that could involve him. But Loveday could be right. Having a chat with Rupe Caine might not be a bad idea.

According to her, the man was pestering Cadan about his gambling debts. It certainly justified a visit. And if he was also able to see his kids, then that would be no bad thing.

Other thoughts were crowding in. They would have to speak to Paxton-Quinn again, assuming that is, that they could find him. He would also like to interview Sabine De Fries, although he wasn't quite sure of the justification for doing that. As far as he knew, she had done nothing wrong. The fact that Cassie's friends were gossiping about the woman's possible involvement in gambling was just that — gossip.

He took a deep breath. It was like following the twists and turns of a maze. When the Langley sketches came to light they had brought Billy Travis back in for questioning. He'd admitted knowing about them, but denied he'd been aware that they had any value. They didn't believe him, of course, but without evidence to the contrary they were forced to release him again.

Loveday stirred next to him and he turned to watch her sleeping. Her long dark hair was tousled, and there was a half-smile on her lips. Sam leaned across and gently moved the strands of hair from her face. After Tessa, he'd promised himself never to let any woman get this close to him again, and he'd meant it. Loveday had just kind of sneaked up on him. And now here he was, totally bowled over by her.

He closed his eyes, but it was some time before sleep eventually took over.

★ ★ ★

It was the brightness in the room that woke Loveday next morning. She blinked, raising her arms in a luxurious stretch before she realized that Sam was not there beside her. She sprang out of bed, reaching for her thick towelling robe and slipped it on as she padded into the kitchen.

Sam was standing by the open door, gazing out in dismay. The drive had disappeared and both their cars were now just large bumps in the snow.

'Oh . . . ' Loveday said, following his gaze to the deserted road. 'Does this mean you won't be going into the station today?'

'Not unless you have a set of skis tucked away somewhere.'

Across the way, Loveday saw Cassie's kitchen door slowly open as Adam, in pyjamas and dressing-gown, peered blearily out. She heard him curse.

'I know,' Sam called across to him. 'A bugger, isn't it?'

Adam frowned, trying to remember

how many spades and shovels he had in his shed.

An hour later, after they had washed the sleep from their eyes and had some breakfast inside them, the four adults, plus Sophie and little Leo, trudged outside to start shovelling snow. In contrast to the previous day, the sky was periwinkle-blue, and a low sun made the snow sparkle like a carpet of glittering diamonds.

'Seems a shame to move it,' Cassie remarked.

Loveday looked up, laughing, and pointed to the children in their bright yellow boots and macs, who had already got busy with buckets and spades.

Sam squinted down at them, grinning.

'I think we should all get shovelling before these two put us to shame.'

They were still in high spirits by the time they had cleared almost halfway down the drive. Loveday put a hand on her back and stretched, glancing at the results of their efforts. They had dug both cars out of the snow and cleared the area between the cottage and the big house.

The snowplough had been out and a narrow track had been cleared along the main road, allowing vehicles to get on the move.

'I think we've all earned a break,' Cassie said, beckoning Loveday to come indoors and help make some coffee.

In the big, warm kitchen that smelled deliciously of roasting meat, they set mugs on a tray, filled a plastic bowl with biscuits, and poured beakers of juice for the children.

Cassie glanced to the window, a wistful smile on her face.

'You're enjoying this, aren't you?' Loveday grinned.

Her friend wheeled round. 'Aren't you?'

'Yes,' Loveday said softly, watching Sam stand up and wipe his brow, 'I am.'

By noon, they had cleared a wide enough path to allow their vehicles access to and from the road.

Adam put a hand on Sam's shoulder. 'Fancy a snifter? I've a bottle of medicinal malt in my study.'

Sam thought of the drive back to Truro

and began to shake his head.

'Go on,' Loveday laughed. 'One small drink won't do you any harm.'

'Who said anything about a small one?' Adam joked.

Sam frowned. 'I suppose I could give the station a call ... find out what's happening. I doubt if very much traffic will be moving today.'

'Now you're talking, Sam,' Cassie called over to them. 'I'm expecting you two to do full justice to my Sunday roast. It's been cooking slowly in the oven for the past hour or so, and it'll be on the table in the blink of an eye.'

She put up a hand when she saw Sam was about to refuse. 'And I won't be taking no for an answer.'

Sam gave a slow smile and put an arm around Loveday, drawing her close. 'Thanks, Cassie. I can't think of anything I would enjoy more.'

*   *   *

It was late Sunday afternoon when Sam left for Truro. Will and Malcolm were in the CID room. Paxton Quinn still hadn't turned up and the search for him had drawn a blank.

A further search on Sabine De Fries threw up no new information. He could hardly arrest her for knowing Merrick's brother.

Sam shuffled the papers on his desk, got up, and went to the window. It was dark now, and although the roads were black, snow still glistened from the rooftops.

There had been nothing in the files on Cadan, either; apparently he had no criminal past, at least not officially. That didn't mean he had nothing to hide. Sam remembered how bitter he had been when Edward Tremayne had bypassed him to entrust his beloved magazine to Merrick. It had been the right decision; Sam was in no doubt that *Cornish Folk* would long since have gone to the wall if Cadan had been left in charge.

Cadan had refused the offer of an executive post on the magazine. He'd wanted to be in sole charge of the business, but that was never going to happen — Edward Tremayne was far too wily for that. The whole thing had ended badly with Cadan abandoning his long-time girlfriend, Ginny Lancaster, and taking off in his black Alfa Romeo. And now he was back!

Sam frowned. The man was up to no good, he was sure of that. He was out to cause trouble for Merrick. It was quite possible that he had stolen Edward's painting, or arranged to have it stolen. He went over in his head what Loveday had told him about following Cadan to Sabine De Fries' boutique in Falmouth. And if Sabine was the woman he'd seen visiting Quinn, well . . .

His head was throbbing. He stared out at the snowy roofs and wondered what Jack and Maddie were doing now. It had been three weeks since he'd seen them, although they had spoken on the phone. But it wasn't the same.

He had intended driving to Plymouth the very next weekend he had free, and taking Jack and Maddie out for tea . . . Pizza Hut, or maybe McDonald's . . . yes, that's what he would do. But he wouldn't wait for a free weekend. He would do it tomorrow. He would take Loveday's advice and drive to Plymouth to interview Rupe Caine.

14

Loveday glanced down at the large brown envelope on the passenger seat as she drove to the office. She was still uncertain about calling on Sabine again. Sam would no doubt accuse her of interfering, but the woman had a right to know what Cadan Tremayne was really like. And besides, she had the pictures from the photoshoot still to deliver.

She was annoyed with herself for not walking into the boutique on Saturday afternoon, whether Cadan had been there or not, even if her unexpected appearance might not have been appreciated.

She had to admit, though, that whatever kind of relationship the pair had, it was intriguing — not to mention, something of a coincidence. The more she considered it, the more she accepted that the glamorous Sabine, with her long silky blonde hair and hypnotic green eyes, was exactly the kind of woman Cadan Tremayne would go for. Someone should warn her that the man wasn't to be trusted. Loveday just wasn't looking forward to being the one to break the bad news.

She had been so deep in thought that the journey to Truro had passed in a flash. Before she knew it, she was pulling into the magazine office's staff car park, taking up her space beside Merrick's black Rover.

He had been watching for her, and beckoned her into his office as she entered the editorial suite.

'Shut the door, Loveday,' he said, indicating that she should take the chair across the desk from him.

She gave him a worried look. 'Is something wrong, Merrick?' The question was unnecessary because she could see by his face that something was clearly very wrong.

He glanced out to the office, where Keri was busy on her computer. In the far corner of the room, Mylor had a phone clamped to his ear, but his attention was on the spread of photographs on the desk before him.

'It's about Cadan,' Merrick said. 'I think he might have got himself involved in something serious this time.'

Loveday's heart sank. Did this mean that he would be dragging Sabine down with him? She really would make a point of stopping off at the Falmouth boutique on the way home.

She focused her attention back on Merrick.

'What kind of serious?'

He got up and went to the window, glancing down on the street below where people, muffled in scarfs and tugged-up collars, were picking their way carefully along the icy pavements. 'I think it's drugs,' he said.

Loveday stared at him. 'Drugs?' She hadn't been expecting that. 'You think Cadan is taking drugs?'

Her mind reeled over the last couple of occasions when she'd seen him. There had been nothing about his manner or body language to suggest he was a user. And even if he was, why would Merrick care? Cadan had brought nothing but trouble to the Tremayne family, and now here he was again giving them grief. She felt no compassion for the man, just anger. He was still haranguing Merrick about the ownership of the magazine. Wasn't that enough?

'Don't you think Cadan is old enough to look after himself?' she said stiffly.

Merrick turned back to his desk and dropped wearily into his chair. 'No, not this time. I don't actually think that he can.'

'How do you mean?'

Merrick paused before speaking, choosing his words carefully. 'Cadan plays the roulette wheel. He owes money . . . a great deal of money . . . to a casino in Plymouth.'

Loveday nodded. 'Rupe Caine, yes. I know about that.'

'You know?'

'Well, assumed, really . . . Mrs Bishop mentioned something about the telephone calls he'd been getting from Caine.'

'Ah, Connie. Yes, she said you were out at the house.' He gave her a disapproving frown. 'We still need to talk about that.'

Loveday glanced away, her cheeks reddening. She cleared her throat. 'How much money are we talking about, Merrick?'

'I've only overheard snippets of phone conversations he's had with this man, but I think we could be talking five figures.'

'What!' Loveday gulped. 'Are you sure? How on earth did he manage to run up a debt like that?'

Merrick's shoulders sagged and he shook his head. 'It gets worse. I think this individual is forcing Cadan to smuggle drugs into the country.'

Loveday stared at him. She could feel her anger rising. How much more damage could this man do? 'Don't you think you should leave him to get out of this by himself?' She could hear her voice was rising but she was powerless to stop it. 'For heaven's sake, Merrick, I know Cadan's your brother, but it's only a few days since he was plotting to steal the magazine from right under your nose.' She shook her head. 'And still you want to help him . . . ?'

Merrick sighed. 'I know. Crazy, isn't it?'

he said. 'But this is different. It would kill the old man if he ever got to hear of this.'

Loveday leaned forward. 'Have you told Sam about this?'

'God, no. I don't want Sam involved. Besides, I've no proof of what I've just told you.' He looked up at her. 'And I don't want this going any further.'

'That goes without saying, but I don't really see how I can help.'

'Well at the moment nor can I, but I trust your judgement, Loveday.' He shrugged. 'I just thought that maybe if we put our heads together we might come up with something.'

'Oh, Merrick.' He looked so desolate that she had to force herself from getting up and putting her arms around him. Out in the office, Keri and Mylor were beginning to take an interest in their conversation. She caught Keri's eye and forced a cheerful smile, but she doubted if that would be enough to throw her savvy little friend off the tracks.

Out in the office the phones were already beginning to ring constantly.

'I should get back out there, Merrick,'

she said apologetically.

'What? Oh, of course.' He sounded miles away. 'Don't mind me.'

Loveday got up to leave, and then turned back. 'We *will* sort this, Merrick. I promise you.'

He gave her a stiff smile and nodded. 'Of course we will.'

But all morning, Loveday's attention was continually drawn back to Merrick's dejected figure on the other side of the glass partition. Seeing him like this was worrying.

She felt guilty keeping this new information from Sam. She hadn't heard from him that day, but she presumed he had gone to Plymouth to interview the casino owner. She frowned, thinking. She had to put him in the picture about Cadan. It was important.

Her eyes slid up to the ceiling. If she could find whatever it was that Cadan had been searching for, then it might provide some of the answers to this problem. She glanced at the clock. It was after ten, and she had a heap of work to tackle before lunchtime. Her visit back up to the file room wouldn't be happening today.

The rest of the morning flew past as Loveday put the finishing touches to two new articles, and sorted out with Mylor the photographs that would go with them. When Keri asked if she was joining her at the café next door for their usual coffee and sandwiches, Loveday shook her head.

'Sorry, Keri, too busy today; but be a love and bring something back for me.'

She knew Keri was giving her a funny look, but she wasn't up to fabricating a story about her earlier chat with Merrick. He had already left for a lunch appointment, and when Keri went out, Loveday was alone in the office.

She got up and walked to the window, stretching as she looked out over Lemon Quay. It was busy with lunchtime shoppers. Christmas was only days away, and everyone but her seemed to be getting organized. She suddenly had an overwhelming longing to be home in Scotland.

Her parents' pub in the Black Isle, just

outside Inverness, would be packed with customers right now. She could picture her dad behind the bar pulling pints, and her mum hurrying back and forth from the kitchen, carrying plates piled high with her homemade steak pie and chips.

Loveday rested her forehead on the cold glass and felt a tear sting her eye. She was tired . . . that was what this sudden wave of nostalgia was about.

Her mobile began to trill and she turned back to her desk to pick it up.

It was Sam. 'Hello, you,' he said. 'I've taken your advice. I'm in Plymouth.'

'Really?' Loveday perched on the desk. It was as though fate was taking a hand. 'Have you spoken to Rupe Caine yet?'

'Not yet,' Sam hedged, unwilling to admit he had driven all this way and the man he'd come to interview was away in Switzerland. But he could hardly have made an appointment.

'That's good,' Loveday said quickly, 'because I have something to tell you, and I know you will treat this sensitively.'

'Yes . . . ?' Sam said warily.

'It's about Merrick's brother; and I

don't mean about the gambling thing, there's more.' She took a deep breath. 'Look, Sam. Merrick told this to me in confidence, but I'm worried for him, and ... well, it's all going to come out anyway.

'Merrick thinks Cadan is being forced to smuggle drugs in from the Continent. It's just a feeling he has, I mean, it's possible he's been putting two and two together and making five, but he's got it into his head that this casino owner in Plymouth has been putting pressure on Cadan to settle his debts, and ... '

'And he's talked him into settling up by getting involved in a spot of drug-running?' Sam finished her sentence, his expression grim.

Loveday nodded.

'That's about the gist of it.'

'Leave it with me, Loveday,' he said thoughtfully, clicking off the connection and staring back at the garishly-painted Red Dragon casino.

★ ★ ★

Sabine was slipping the delicate silk negligee her customer had just purchased into one of the boutique's elegant black bags when she spotted Loveday coming along the road. She froze for a split second, wondering why she'd come back, when she spotted the large brown envelope in her hand.

By the time the customer had left and Loveday had entered the boutique, Sabine had her welcoming smile ready.

Loveday wafted the envelope at her. 'The proofs . . . I said I'd bring them.'

Sabine turned to the stylish, dark-haired woman who was re-arranging the window display, and called out as she directed Loveday through to the back room: 'Can you keep an eye on things, Francine?'

The woman slid a look at Loveday and gave a brief nod.

'Francine is a friend who helps me out now and again,' Sabine explained as they moved into the stockroom.

On the table by the window that looked out over Falmouth Harbour, a collection of white porcelain mugs vied for space with an open ledger. Dusk was already falling, and the lights from the foreshore were playing dancing patterns on the water below. Further out, Loveday could see boats bobbing at their moorings, and wondered if Sabine had her own little tender tied up down there.

Sabine was looking at the photographs Loveday had spread out on the table when Francine popped her head round the door. 'Sorry to interrupt, but there's someone to see you. He says it's important.'

Loveday thought she'd caught a flash of alarm in Sabine's green eyes as she dropped the photo she had been examining back onto the table and gave both women a dazzling smile.

'I was about to make Miss Ross a cup of coffee. Could you do the honours, Francine?' she said, as she swept out of the room.

Loveday could hear the murmur of voices from the boutique as Sabine and her visitor conducted their exchange in subdued tones. Whatever they were talking about, neither one wanted to be overheard.

'Sabine is much in demand today. I

suppose she has these reps calling in all the time.'

It was a clumsy attempt to pump Francine for information, but there had been something about that fleetingly fearful look that had intrigued Loveday.

'He isn't a rep,' Francine said, looking through the photos. 'He's an associate.'

Loveday's experience as a journalist had taught her that sometimes staying silent prompted the other person to speak. She waited.

'I suppose this means Sabine will be off to Amsterdam again,' Francine said.

But before Loveday had a chance to question that, Sabine was back.

'Now then, where were we?' she said, casting her eye over the table.

'I've made the coffee,' Francine said.

'Frankie, you're an angel.' Sabine gestured for Loveday to help herself.

The shop bell tinkled and they all looked towards the boutique.

'I'd better see to that,' Francine said, moving off.

Sabine turned her attention back to the photographs.

'Are these the ones you've chosen?'

'Well, yes,' Loveday began. 'But if you particularly like any of these others, I'm sure Merrick will have an open mind.'

'Merrick?'

'My boss, Merrick Tremayne. He owns the magazine.' She paused, sliding Sabine a glance. She still wasn't sure she should get involved here. What did it matter to her who the woman was seeing? But a niggling twinge in the back of her mind was telling her it wasn't fair to leave her in ignorance about Cadan. She took a breath and continued, 'I think you know Merrick's brother . . . Cadan Tremayne?'

For a split-second she thought Sabine was going to deny it, but instead she wrinkled her beautiful straight nose. 'Do I?'

'I'm sorry; it's none of my business. It's just that . . . well, I saw you with him the other day.'

Sabine narrowed her green eyes and turned away, reaching for one of the pictures Loveday had pushed aside.

'Could we use this one?'

Loveday glanced at the proof. It wasn't

261

one of the best, and she suspected the woman didn't care one way or the other if they used it or not. She was clearly dismissing the subject of Cadan. But why?

Loveday was beginning to regret that she'd mentioned him. Apparently, the subject of Merrick's brother was strictly out of bounds. She'd been about to gather up the proofs and leave when Sabine turned, her steady green gaze fixed on Loveday's face. 'Why were you asking about Cadan?'

Loveday swallowed. 'I'm sorry . . . forgive me. I shouldn't have mentioned him.'

'But you have, and now I would like to know why.'

Loveday wasn't sure how much she should say.

'Cadan has . . . a reputation,' she began slowly, selecting her words with care.

Sabine lifted her coffee mug, her gaze never leaving Loveday's face.

'What kind of reputation?' she asked quietly.

'He . . . well, he gambles.' She paused,

uncertain if she should go on, but she had started now and it was too late to go back. She straightened her shoulders.

'Look, Sabine. I like you, and I'm only mentioning this because I don't want to see you getting hurt. Cadan has substantial gambling debts.'

'I'm listening.'

Loveday took a deep breath. 'So he'll be looking for someone to bail him out.'

Sabine was staring at her. There was a glint of tears in her eyes. 'You think he's using me?' Her voice was tremulous.

Loveday reached across to touch the woman's arm. 'I could be wrong,' she said gently. 'All I'm saying is, watch your step with him.'

Sabine was holding her head in her hands. 'I don't believe this. Cadan is a lovely man. You must have got this wrong.' She swallowed. 'You're saying he owes money to a casino? What casino . . . where?'

Loveday told her about Rupe Caine.

Sabine reached for a chair and sank onto it.

Loveday could hear the shop door

tinkle . . . another customer. She glanced out over the dark rippling water, and towards the lights of the harbour. A large tanker was slowly manoeuvring itself alongside one of the quays.

She couldn't just walk out and leave Sabine like this. She could picture her jumping in her car and driving like fury to Merrick's house to confront Cadan.

She'd dropped herself right in it now. She'd done what her friends — what Sam — were always warning her against. She'd interfered.

'I'm sorry, Sabine,' she sighed. 'I just didn't want you to be taken in by him. He's just not worth it.'

'No . . . no, you're right. I needed to know this.' Sabine reached out to take Loveday's hand. 'I'm more grateful to you than you'll ever know,' she said quietly.

The words rang in Loveday's head as she drove home. Another worry was niggling somewhere in the back of her mind; but, try as she might, she couldn't recall it. She knew it was useless trying to force it. It would come back to her . . . eventually.

15

There had been no sign of Rupe Caine at the Red Dragon Casino. An ugly-looking doorman of ape-like proportions relented under Sam's hard stare and grudgingly scribbled down an address, adding with a sneer that a visit was pointless as Caine had flown to Geneva on business that very morning.

Sam cursed under his breath as he walked back to his car. He would definitely still see his kids, but as far as meeting the casino owner was concerned the trip to Plymouth was looking like a wasted journey.

He took out the note and glanced at the scrawled address. He knew the area. A wealthy farmer with land on the south side of the city had somehow inveigled his way through council planning, and secured consent to build six luxury homes on his vast farming estate.

On impulse, Sam started the engine and drove out to the city's suburbs. A set of high wrought-iron gates barred his way into Caine's property. Bringing the Lexus to a halt directly under the surveillance camera, he rolled down the window and held up his warrant card.

To his surprise the gates swung open. He spotted the dark green Porsche at once, and parked alongside it. The elegant period villa with its sweeping lawns was a gentleman's home, except Rupe Caine was no gentleman. Sam was beginning to wonder if he'd been deliberately given a wrong address, when a voice from behind him bellowed, 'Who the hell are you?'

Sam spun round and saw a small, slight figure striding towards him. He couldn't have been more than fifty, but his grey hair was already thinning, and the pale blue eyes were not looking at all friendly.

'Detective Inspector Sam Kitto,' Sam said quietly, pulling out his warrant card. 'I've come to see Rupert Caine?'

'Well, you've found him,' Caine snapped. 'Now what do you want?'

'Perhaps we could we step inside, sir?'

Caine gave an irritated sigh. 'I have a plane to catch, so you'll have to be brief, Inspector.'

Sam followed him into a large farm-house kitchen, where the walls were lined with expensive-looking oak units. A dining table and eight chairs sat by patio doors that looked out to the garden. The gleaming dark green Aga looked as though it had never been used.

'We'll use my study,' Caine said brusquely. 'It's through here.'

They crossed a reception hall, where a wide balustrade staircase swept up to a higher floor, and went into a small room.

Rupe Caine settled himself behind a large desk and motioned Sam to the armchair in the corner.

'So, Inspector, how can I help you?'

'Cadan Tremayne,' Sam said bluntly, and saw the man's eyes twitch. 'One of your customers, I believe.'

'Maybe,' Caine said hesitantly. His gaze was more wary now.

'No 'maybe' about it, sir. I know he owes you money.'

Caine shrugged. 'If you know that, then why are you asking? Is he in some sort of trouble?'

Sam gave him an innocent stare. 'Word

is, you've been threatening him.' He was in no position yet to accuse the man of drug-running, but neither did he intend to give him an easy time.

'He stole from me,' he said. 'Nobody does that.'

Sam fought to control his surprise. 'What did he steal?'

'Nothing I can prove — not yet, anyway, but I know it was him.' He pointed to a bare wall. 'A painting by an old Cornish artist used to hang there. It mysteriously disappeared two days after Cadan sat where you are now, Inspector.'

Sam frowned. 'I still don't see why you would assume it was him, especially as you say you have no proof.'

'I'm working on that.' The malice in Caine's pale eyes set Sam's teeth on edge. Despite his lack of stature, there was an air of menace about the man.

'If your property has been burgled, sir, then it's a police matter. I presume you have reported it?'

'Of course,' Caine said quickly.

But the man's response came too fast to be convincing. If he was into drugs, as

Merrick suspected, he wouldn't want any smart young detectives with their eyes on promotion rooting about in his business. But that was exactly what was going to happen, and sooner rather than later.

Caine glanced at his watch. 'Look, time's getting on, so if you have no more questions, Inspector . . . ' He made a gesture, indicating it was time for Sam to leave.

In the hall, Sam's eyes went to the artwork on the white walls. He was no expert, but he knew enough to tell these were all original paintings by obviously talented artists.

'You have excellent taste, Mr Caine.'

Rupe's eyes followed Sam's gaze to the pictures.

'I suspect we both know that is not true. None of these were my choice. They were selected for me by . . . ' He hesitated. 'By a friend.' His voice faltered, and he cleared his throat.

For the first time, Sam saw a spark of emotion in the icy blue eyes. He was obviously talking about a woman. 'Sounds like you and this friend were close,' he said.

'We were.' Caine's voice was clipped. 'When she lived here, we were very close.'

Sam would have liked to ask more, but the man's expression told him the subject was now closed.

'Well, if that's all, Inspector,' Caine said, moving to hold the door open. Sam strode through, turning back at the last moment.

'That painting you had stolen, sir . . . who was the artist?'

'It was a Wallis,' Rupe Caine said crisply. 'An Alfred Wallis.'

Sam started, hoping his expression was bland enough to hide his mounting excitement. He nodded to Caine. 'Thank you for your time, sir,' he said evenly, as the door closed quickly behind him.

For a few moments he sat in his car going over what he had just been told. Two valuable stolen paintings by the same artist — and Cadan Tremayne's name mentioned in connection with each one. But why would Cadan steal works of art, if not to raise money to clear his gambling debts and get Rupe Caine off his back?

If that were the case it would make no sense for him to steal from the man himself. So surely that meant that Cadan hadn't been involved in the thefts after all. Or had he?

★ ★ ★

It was dark as Sam drove back to Cornwall, but all in all it had been a good day. Jack and Maddie's excitement at seeing him again always brought a lump to his throat. It would still be hard when he knew they were flying off to Florida with Victoria and her fancy man, but at least now there was something new to look forward to.

Jack had given him an uncertain look as he munched on the biggest cheeseburger Sam had ever seen. 'You don't mind us going to Florida with Matt, do you, Dad?' He clearly thought he did.

Sam's heart gave a lurch as he turned and met his son's troubled brown eyes. He hadn't been expecting that. He'd been angry that this stranger was taking his family away for Christmas when it should have been him. But that would hardly have been possible. He'd felt a rush of shame at the thought of his own selfishness. His kids deserved to have a good time, even if he wasn't the one providing it.

He spread his arms and drew the children close. 'Of course I don't mind. You'll have a wonderful time.' He pulled back and waggled a finger. 'Just don't forget, I'll be expecting to see hundreds of pictures. I'll want to know about *everything*.'

'I wish you could come, too, Daddy,' Maddie said, her eyes bright with unshed tears.

Sam had to swallow the lump in his throat. 'D'you know what,' he said. 'Why don't we have our own special holiday after Christmas — maybe early next year when you break up for half-term?'

Maddie looked up at him, eyes wide. 'Could we really, Daddy?' She was clearly excited at this new plan. 'Could we go to LEGOLAND?'

'I want to go to London — to the Science Museum,' Jack said firmly.

Maddie's bottom lip came out defiantly. 'LEGOLAND,' she insisted.

Sam put up his hands, laughing. 'Why don't we do both?'

He was still smiling at the memory as he crossed the Tamar Bridge back into Cornwall. He'd had that precious time with his children, and managed to slip two very large boxes — Christmas gifts he had bought for them before turning up at the house — to Victoria, for safekeeping until the big day.

His meeting with Rupe Caine had also given him much to think about. For Merrick's sake, Sam was hoping Cadan hadn't been involved in those art thefts.

He was on the A30, driving through the blackness of Bodmin Moor, when his thoughts drifted back to Jago Tilley and why he'd hidden his mother's picture in his neighbour's garden shed.

The only possible conclusion was that Jago had thought the picture was in danger of being stolen. Could there be a connection here that he hadn't even thought of?

Billy Travis would have been the main

suspect in any theft from Jago's cottage, and he was also quite capable of burgling Merrick's home and stealing the painting. But then he would have to have known the painting was there, and worth stealing. That thought brought Sam back to Cadan.

He was still considering the possibility of Cadan's involvement in his investigation as he pulled into his drive, and frowned at the light he could see on in his sitting-room.

His front door opened as he got out of the car, and Loveday was standing there, silhouetted in the light.

'You did tell me to make myself at home,' she said sheepishly.

Sam threw his arms wide and gathered her into them. 'You've no idea how pleased I am to see you,' he said, before he kissed her.

16

Maisie and Agnes, the magazine's two cleaning ladies, were still finishing off their work, and looked up in surprise at Loveday's early arrival. She'd been determined to get into the office before any of her colleagues to give herself a chance to root about in the file room upstairs.

It wouldn't matter if the cleaners knew what she was doing, they would hardly be interested. But she was wrong, for a pair of worried eyes followed her across the editorial floor, and out to the stairs.

Loveday surveyed the dusty rows of filing cabinets with dismay. It could take weeks to go through every single one, especially as she had no idea what she was looking for. She needed a plan. She began working from left to right, giving each cabinet a number in her notebook, ticking each one off as she finished going through it.

She'd been so engrossed in her search that she didn't hear the door open, and turned with a start when a hand touched her shoulder. 'Agnes! You nearly gave me a heart attack. What are you doing up here?'

Agnes Dobell wiped clammy hands on her blue nylon overall and bit her lip to stop it trembling. 'What you're looking for,' she said. 'It isn't here.'

Loveday stared at her. 'You don't know what I'm looking for.'

'I do, actually,' Agnes said. 'It's downstairs in the cleaning cupboard.'

Intrigued, Loveday followed the woman back downstairs, and stood back uncertainly as Agnes unlocked the cupboard door and reached up to the top shelf. She pulled out a manila envelope. 'It's all here,' she said.

Loveday took the envelope and, with a confused frown, eased it open. The document inside didn't make any sense.

Her mind reeled back to the day she'd found Cadan rifling through the files. She was remembering the slight figure that had ducked into a shop doorway as she

276

left the magazine office.

'It was you,' she said, staring at Agnes. 'You were there that day?'

⋆ ⋆ ⋆

Sam spent the first hour of the morning briefing his team about his previous day's interview with Rupe Caine.

Will frowned. 'I'm not clear what any of this has to do with the Jago Tilley murder, boss?'

Sam sighed. 'It's only a gut feeling, but we're not in a position to ignore any possible link.'

'You think Cadan Tremayne could be involved in all this?' Amanda said, her voice registering her surprise.

Sam pushed aside some files on his desk and slid his hip onto it. 'I'm not ruling him out of the art thefts. Caine was certainly convinced Cadan stole his painting.'

'If that's the case, why isn't he dead?' Amanda said.

She had a point. The casino owner's fury at the man had certainly been obvious. But then, that could have been because Cadan had refused to bring drugs into the country for him, as Merrick had suspected. He'd thought long and hard before deciding not to confront Rupe Caine with that accusation — not yet, anyway. There was more digging to be done.

And besides, maybe Cadan was more use to him alive than dead. Sam could only hope that was the case. In the meantime, he and Amanda would call on Cadan Tremayne. He had a few things to say to Merrick's brother.

He turned to Will. 'I want you to get on to the Met's Art and Antiques Unit, Will, see if they can shed any light on our stolen paintings. They have a database in London of stolen artwork, antiques and the like.'

'Right, boss,' Will nodded.

'What would you like me to do, sir?' Malcolm Carter asked.

'Can you give the boys in blue in Plymouth a ring? I didn't get a chance to call in there yesterday.' If Malcolm thought it strange that his boss went all the way to Plymouth to interview a local rogue, and didn't see fit to call in at the local nick, he showed no sign of it.

'Anything they have on Rupe Caine would be good. He said he reported the theft of his painting, but I very much doubt that. You might also run Cadan Tremayne's name past them, see if he's known to them.'

Sam waved an arm in Amanda's direction. 'You're with me, DC Fox. We have a call to pay on young Tremayne.'

Amanda hurried after Sam as he strode out of the CID suite, making for the stairs and the car park.

'We'll take one of the pool cars. You can drive.'

He saw her surprised glance. He knew he'd probably be taking his life in his hands with Amanda at the wheel, but he needed to think.

Connie Bishop opened the door after the first knock. 'Merrick's at the office, Mr Kitto,' she said, her eyes sliding to Amanda.

'It's Cadan we've come to see, Connie. Is he here?'

She looked surprised. 'Um, yes, I'll give him a call,' she said, stepping aside to allow them in. 'If you just wait in there.' She nodded towards the front room. 'I'll fetch him down.'

But she didn't have to do any fetching, for Cadan, in a purple patterned shirt and dark cords, was coming down the stairs.

'Sam. How nice.' He smiled, his eyes on Amanda. 'And you've brought a little friend.'

Sam waited until he had come into the room and Connie had left, closing the door behind her. 'We're making enquiries about a stolen painting,' he said. 'I understand you are acquainted with a certain casino owner in Plymouth by the name of Rupe Caine?'

There was no need for a response, because the colour had drained from Cadan's face as he went to the fire and stood with his back to the two officers. 'Who says I know him?'

'Mr Caine says so. In fact, he said a lot more than that when I spoke to him yesterday.' Sam paused for a moment, allowing the implications of this to sink in. 'He said you stole his painting.'

Cadan spun round, his expression one of indignant outrage. 'He's mistaken. I know nothing about a stolen painting.'

Sam gave a slow smile and pursed his lips. 'Well, you see, Cadan, it's a funny thing . . . ' He paused, drawing out the tension. ' . . . but the picture that was taken from here, and the one Caine claims has been stolen from his home in Plymouth, are by the same artist. Now, either that's a huge coincidence, or somebody is starting an illegal collection of Alfred Wallis's work.' He met Cadan's eyes. 'Wouldn't you say?'

Cadan was pacing the room now, rubbing the back of his neck. 'Okay, I owe Caine some money, I'll put my hands up to that, but I didn't steal his bloody picture. He's got it in for me because he knows I can't pay him at the moment . . . bit of a cash-flow problem.' He gave Sam and Amanda a nervous smile. 'It's only temporary.'

Sam fixed him with a look. 'Has Rupe Caine asked you to bring drugs into the country for him?'

Cadan reached for a chair and sat down. 'You know I can't answer that. Have you met that gorilla he keeps at the casino?'

Sam nodded. 'We're acquainted.'

'Then you'll know why I can't answer your questions, Sam.'

'I'll take that as a yes, then,' Sam said.

Cadan put his head in his hands. 'If you tell Caine I admitted that, then I'm a dead man.'

'This isn't going away, Cadan,' Sam said, more quietly this time. 'You will have to speak to us some time. And for your sake, it had better be soon.'

* * *

Merrick stared at the document Loveday had just handed him. 'Where did you get this?'

'You wouldn't believe it if I told you; but I'm right, aren't I? That letter definitely states that your father left the magazine to Cadan.'

Merrick's brows knitted. 'But he didn't.'

'No, but somebody has gone to a lot of trouble to make it appear so.' She jabbed a finger at the page. 'Oliver Kilpatrick . . . he's your solicitor, isn't he?'

Merrick scratched his head. 'I have a document identical to this, except it's my name there, and not Cadan's.' He looked up and met her excited eyes. 'What's going on, Loveday?'

Loveday glanced out to the office, to where Keri was sliding suspicious glances in their direction.

She paused, taking a deep breath. 'Agnes Dobell is one of our cleaning ladies — you know, the younger, pretty one.'

Merrick nodded.

'When the legal documents were drawn up transferring the magazine to you, Agnes worked as a temp in Oliver Kilpatrick's office.' Loveday paused again, studying Merrick's shocked face as the implication of this began to sink in. She continued, 'Cadan had been leading her on, and she had a crush on him. Now, Agnes was no stranger to computers, and I know this sounds ridiculous, but she devised a plan to get into his good books.'

'Okay,' Merrick said. 'What did she do?'

Loveday tapped the papers on his desk. 'She forged this version of the transfer schedule, substituting Cadan's name for yours as the new owner of the magazine.'

Merrick picked up the document, waving it in Loveday's face. 'But this is my signature at the bottom. She couldn't have forged that.'

'She didn't have to, she just slipped the counterfeit one in amongst the real transfer documents for you to sign, trusting that you wouldn't read each one in detail.'

Merrick raised his hand. 'I still don't understand. Why is this only coming to light now?'

'Simple,' said Loveday. 'Agnes got cold feet at the last minute and took the altered paper home with her. Cadan didn't know a thing about it. But they met by chance a few weeks ago ... I don't know the details, but Agnes ended up telling Cadan she knew how he could take over the magazine. You see, she'd hung on to that fake document.'

Merrick gave Loveday an incredulous stare. 'Agnes Dobell! We're talking about little Agnes Dobell?'

Loveday nodded.

Merrick's face was a picture of incredulity. 'So why didn't Cadan get his hands on this?'

'Because Agnes chickened out again. She'd told Cadan the fake transfer document was hidden in one of the filing cabinets upstairs, but apparently her fear of being found out was greater than her infatuation for him, and she retrieved the document before he got to it.'

'And she just gave this to you? But why?'

'She found me rummaging about in the file room, and worked out what I was looking for. It was that old fear thing again.' Loveday stared at Merrick's shocked face. 'I thought you'd be pleased.'

The appalled expression broke into a smile. 'Pleased? I'm elated. I can't tell you how much I appreciate this.' He was tempted to get up, cross the room and hug her, but the sight of Keri's suspicious glance stopped him.

'What happens now?' Loveday asked. 'Will you sack Agnes?'

Merrick shook his head. 'I'll speak to her, of course, but what purpose would it serve to sack her? She's owned up to what she did.'

★　★　★

It was just after lunchtime before Sam got the chance to catch up with Will again. He beckoned him into his office.

'What happened with the art fraud boys, Will? Did you come up with anything?'

Will screwed up his face. 'Yes and no. They had old man Tremayne's painting on their list, but not Rupe Caine's.'

'So, what's the 'yes' part?'

'Well, it might be nothing, at least not as far as our murder investigation goes, but apparently there's been a pattern of stolen artwork over the past two or three years. Break-ins at small galleries all over Europe. Never anything from the major museums and galleries, presumably because they have better security.'

'How do you mean, *pattern*?'

'These thefts the art squad are investigating come in spates.' He paused, working out the best way to explain it. 'The thing is, each spate seems to involve work by one particular artist. For instance, a whole bunch of Monet paintings was stolen over a twelve-month period two years ago, and then a couple of works by Pissarro.'

Sam nodded. 'Both of those artists were French. Does your art squad place any significance in that?'

Will shrugged. 'Who knows — but the point is, we now have two paintings by Alfred Wallis stolen in this part of the world. That's kind of a pattern, isn't it? Well, at least the art boys thought so.'

'They're not suggesting these paintings were stolen by the same person?' Sam asked.

'Not necessarily *by* the same person, but maybe *for* the same person,' Will said, looking pleased with himself.

Sam gave an incredulous laugh. 'So now we have an international art thief working in Cornwall? Isn't that just a bit far-fetched?' He was imagining what Loveday would make of this theory.

Will looked crestfallen. 'Yeah, you're right, boss. Put like that, it does seem a bit daft.'

Sam agreed; but there was still the coincidence of those two Alfred Wallis paintings. The pictures the old St Ives fisherman painted were naïve and quirky, and mostly of local scenes. The works were undoubtedly collectors' items, but did Wallis's reputation stretch as far as the Continent?

Sam was now convinced that Paxton-Quinn was in this up to his ears. Why else had he disappeared? He'd had uniformed officers checking all the possible leads to the man's whereabouts, but he still hadn't been found.

He slapped his knee. 'Let's have another go at rooting this bloke out.' He reached for his coat. 'Come on, Will. You're with me.'

Half an hour later they were standing outside a shabby shop on Hale's waterfront. Uniformed officers had already visited the establishment in pursuit of

Quinn, but had drawn a blank.

' 'Vane's Bygones',' Will muttered, staring up at the shop name. 'More like 'long-gones' if this stuff in the window is anything to go by.' It was a far cry from Zachariah Paxton-Quinn's upmarket St Ives gallery. 'Are you sure we've got the right place, boss?'

Sam was wondering the same thing, but it was the only shop in the road that sold this kind of stuff.

A bell above the door tinkled as they went in. The place smelled damp and dusty, as if it was in need of a good clean. Sam would have been loath to touch any of the stuff on display, let alone buy anything.

A short, stockily-built man, wearing an irritated expression and a shabby grey cardigan that was holed at the elbows, shuffled through from the back. His straggly grey hair lent to his general unkempt appearance. Sam wondered what the dapper Paxton-Quinn could possibly have in common with this person.

'If you're just nosing around, then don't be long. I've got a chip pan on through the back,' the man sniffed.

Sam had a sudden image of the thing overheating and bursting into flames, and fire licking through this place in an instant. He suppressed a shudder.

'I should turn it off, if I were you,' Sam said, taking out his warrant card and showing it to the man.

'Okay, what d'ye want wi' me?' he grumbled over his shoulder as he shuffled away to do as he'd been told.

'Are you Walter Vane?' Sam asked when he'd returned.

The man's gaze slid from Sam to Will. 'Aye,' he said, suspiciously. 'What of it?'

'We understand you're acquainted with a Mr Zachariah Paxton-Quinn?'

The old man sighed. 'I told the other lot I don't know nothing about him. What's he done, anyway,' he said wearily.

'He appears to have gone missing,' Will cut in.

Walter reached for a chair and sat down heavily, shaking his head. 'Aye well, that much I know. But the other young coppers were keeping their mouths shut about anything else.' He shook his head again. 'Merryn won't be happy to hear about this.'

'Merryn?' Sam repeated.

'My daughter. She's the one that knows him. They had a bit of a thing going after her divorce, but she dumped him. He'd been chasing after this other bit of skirt.' He'd looked up and met Sam's eyes. 'Well, my Merryn wasn't going to put up with that.'

'What did she do?' Sam said.

'It's what she's going to do when she gets back from Paris.'

'And what would that be?' Sam was trying to hold on to his patience.

The old man shrugged. 'How should I know? She doesn't take me into her confidence.' He looked up and gave the detectives a toothless grin. 'You can be sure Quinn won't like it, though.'

At Sam's nod, Will asked, 'Do you know this other woman Quinn was seeing?'

Walter gave another shrug. 'No idea. You'd have to ask Merryn that.'

'Can you tell us where your daughter is staying in Paris?' Will persisted.

Walter shrugged again. 'No idea. Didn't even get a postcard. All I know is that she said she'd be back on the twenty-second.'

'How did she meet Mr Quinn?' Sam asked.

'He just appeared in the shop one day . . . said he was just browsing. It was Merryn that spoke to him.'

Sam handed the old man one of his cards. 'Ring that number if you happen to remember anything more.'

Walter took the card and slipped it into his cardigan pocket. He'd turned, and was beginning to shuffle back to his sanctuary, when Sam said, 'When did your daughter leave for Paris?'

Walter Vane sniffed, and wiped his nose on his ragged sleeve. 'What difference does that make?'

Sam waited, his expression unflinching.

Walter muttered something incoherent to himself, screwing up his eyes. 'Saturday,' he scowled. 'It were last Saturday.'

'What's she doing in Paris, Mr Vane?' Sam asked.

The old man's shoulders heaved into a

shrug. 'How should I know? She don't tell me nothing.'

'Does she go there often?' Sam persisted.

'Couple times a year.' Walter Vane narrowed his eyes at Sam. 'Nothing wrong with that, is there?'

When they got outside, Will turned to his boss. 'That wasn't exactly much help.'

'I'm not sure,' Sam said, wondering now if the absent Merryn had been the woman they'd seen scurrying away from Paxton-Quinn's place in St Ives that day. 'We should run a check on Mr Vane. If I'm right, I think we'll find he's in the same business as our elusive Mr Quinn.'

On the way back to the station, Will said, 'D'you think Quinn is still lying low somewhere in Cornwall?'

Sam shrugged. It was possible. As he saw it, there were two reasons why the man had disappeared. He could have killed old Jago, although — despite the evidence to the contrary — Sam was still favouring Billy Travis for that. Or he could have gone to ground for fear of being arrested for all the other dodgy stuff he was involved in.

There was a third possibility, of course. Sam heaved a deep sigh. He didn't even want to go there.

17

'You won't believe how excited Sophie and Leo are,' Cassie said, breezing into Loveday's kitchen and pulling up a chair.

Loveday reached into the cupboard for another mug. 'How is it that you always know when the kettle's on?' She grinned down at her friend. 'Have you got the place bugged?'

Cassie screwed up her face.

'No . . . but now that you mention it . . . '

'I can just as easily pour this coffee down the sink,' Loveday laughed.

'God, no. Don't do that. I'm desperate. Our kitchen looks like the Blue Peter studio at the moment.'

'The kids have been busy making masks for Montol.' She looked up. 'Are you and Sam coming?'

Loveday was vaguely aware that this was a recently-revived Christmas festival celebrating midwinter, but she knew little more about it.

Cassie sighed.

'For a journalist, you don't know much about what's going on around you.'

It was true. She had been so focused on Jago's murder and helping Priddy that she had been neglecting a lot lately. And now there was this business with Cadan. She hated to see Merrick as worried as he so obviously was. She slid the biscuit tin across the table.

'Okay. I know you're dying to tell me.'

Cassie carefully selected a custard cream and bit into it, flicking the crumbs from the sides of her mouth with her little finger.

'Well, basically Montol is an ancient tradition that's held in this part of Cornwall to celebrate the winter solstice.'

'So what happens?' Loveday asked, taking another sip of coffee.

'It's brilliant,' Cassie said, her eyes lighting up like an excited child's. 'Adam and I went along last year and had such a great time that we wanted to take Sophie and Leo this time.

'The evening kicks off with a lantern procession, starting at various places in the town, and meeting at the highest point, Lescudjack Hillfort.' She looked at Loveday. 'They call it the Rivers of Fire. Don't you think that's great?'

Loveday nodded, and Cassie continued.

'It's wonderful. There's singing and dancing and everyone joins in. Then they all process back down to a big concert in the town centre.' She looked up. 'You and Sam should come.'

'I'll ask him,' Loveday started to say, but Cassie had caught sight of the clock.

'That's never the time? Adam and the kids will think I've emigrated. Did I tell you to wear a mask? Everyone is supposed to wear a Venetian mask. Bring a couple of lanterns, too, if you can get your hands on them,' she called back as she disappeared out the back door.

Loveday stared after her, shaking her head. Where would she get a lantern — never mind a Venetian mask — in twenty-four hours?

★   ★   ★

Time was slipping away, and Sam's team hadn't unearthed another single clue. He didn't want to go to this Montol thing. His children would be on a plane bound for Florida, while he was in Penzance watching silly people messing about. But he'd promised Loveday and he could hardly go back on his word. If it hadn't been for her suggesting he should go to Plymouth to interview Rupe Caine, he wouldn't have seen his children at all before they left.

Penzance was throbbing with excitement when they arrived. Loveday glanced at Sam as they waited in the rapidly growing crowd. She knew he was putting on a brave face, when all he was really thinking about was that Jack and Maddie would be so far away. But what could he do? The fact that his children were so excited about the trip just made the whole thing worse.

Loveday gave his arm a squeeze.

'We can just go and have a quiet drink somewhere, Sam. We don't have to get involved with this.'

People were lighting their lanterns now

and the procession was beginning to move off. Sam tucked her arm into his and bent to peck her cheek.

'No, let's do this. You never know, it might be fun.' His eyes scanned the crowd. 'Are you sure this is where Cassie said they would meet us?'

'Positive,' Loveday nodded. 'They'll be here.'

Almost before the words were out she heard Leo's excited shrill.

'Auntie Love . . . Auntie Love . . . '

Sam shook his head, and in spite of himself managed a grin as Leo and Sophie rushed towards them.

Loveday threw up her hands in mock surprise as she gazed down at the two masked faces.

'Who are you? Do we know you?'

'It's us,' the children squealed in unison, whipping the masks from their faces.

Loveday threw her arms wide and hugged them both.

'You had me completely fooled,' she laughed, glancing up at Cassie and Adam.

'And you've brought Mummy and

299

Daddy with you.'

They both nodded, giving Sam a more guarded smile. He ruffled their hair.

'Great masks, kids. Loveday and I couldn't find any like that in the shops.'

'We didn't buy them,' Sophie announced indignantly. 'We made them.'

Sam raised an eyebrow.

'No way! But they are so beautiful. I don't suppose you made any for Loveday and me?'

The children shook their heads, eyeing him solemnly. Cassie dipped into her bag, produced two more red and gold home-made masks, and handed one to Adam.

'Do I have to?' he protested.

'Absolutely,' Cassie said. 'Just look how jealous Sam and Loveday are already.'

A band had started up, and a dance troupe dressed in flamboyant reds, greens and purples leapt and pranced around the crowds to the beat of the drums. Some people had come prepared, and raised more professional Venetian-style masks to their faces. A cheer went up, as the beating drum grew louder.

More musicians joined the throng, and

the marchers, holding their tealights aloft, moved forward with chants of: 'Montol! Montol!'

Loveday saw Sam frown as his eyes scanned the rows of tea lights, and she gave him a prod. 'Stop being the policeman,' she hissed. 'It's all quite safe.'

Cassie leaned in towards them, her voice coming from behind her big red and purple mask. 'Relax, Sam. Loveday's right. Look at all those marshals.' She pointed to the figures in high-visibility jackets stationed at strategic points along the route. 'The fire service is out in force.'

Sam gave a relenting sigh and put up his hands. 'Okay, I give in,' he grinned, taking Loveday's arm and linking it through his own again.

'This is fun, isn't it,' Cassie said, her eyes shining as she and Adam kept a tight hold on the children, who were bouncing along beside them in time to the music.

The procession had started at various points in the town, but everyone was heading for the ancient hillfort at the highest point. The marchers merged when they reached their destination, and a cheer went up as a beacon was lit.

The music struck up, louder than ever, as more entertainers performed for the crowd in the dancing light of the bonfire beacon.

Then, led by the musicians, the crowd slowly began to move off, guided by the marshalls into a long straggling procession of flickering tealights.

'What happens now?' Sam yelled in Adam's ear.

'It all ends up back in the town centre where there's a ceilidh. We won't be staying for that. Cassie and I will have to get the children home. Not that there'll be much sleeping done tonight, by the look of them.'

Sam glanced down at Sophie and Leo's excited faces, and a wave of nostalgia washed over him. How Jack and Maddie would have loved this.

'You and Loveday should go to the ceilidh,' Cassie added. 'It should be fun.'

Loveday looked up at him and raised a hopeful eyebrow.

Sam sighed, shaking his head and grinning down at her.

'I think that's already been decided.'

When they reached the town centre, the marchers were shepherded around the temporary stage in front of the main hall.

A woman standing next to them suddenly gave a cry of panic as the little Yorkshire terrier she had carried through-out the procession suddenly made a dash for freedom and darted into the dark space at the side of the hall.

'I'll catch him,' Sophie said.

And before anyone could stop her she had shot after the dog.

Loveday put a hand on Cassie's arm.

'I'll go after them. You stay here with the others.'

She hurried forward, aware that Sam was frowning after her.

'Sophie,' she called into the shadows. 'Where are you, Sophie?'

A single, dim bulb cast a pool of weak light on the path, and Loveday let out a relieved gasp as Sophie appeared, the errant dog in her arms.

Aware that Sam had followed her in, Loveday went forward to hurry the child out when something in the bushes caught her eye. She gasped as the realization of what she was seeing swept over her.

'Get Sophie out of here, Loveday,' Sam said sharply — and she knew he had seen it too.

A uniformed police constable was standing at the edge of the crowd and Sam beckoned him over. As the man approached, Sam shouted to Loveday to go home with Cassie.

She waved back her agreement, hurrying Sophie and the little dog back out into the crowd. As they emerged from the side of the hall, Cassie took Leo's hand as she and Adam rushed forward to meet them.

'What is it, Loveday?' Adam kept his voice low.

Loveday glanced back through the shadows. 'I think Sam might need your help, Adam.'

Her heart pounding, she went back with Cassie and the children to the car. She knew her friend would not question her in front of Sophie and Leo. She was torn between the horror of the situation, and relief that the child had not seen what she had.

18

'Adam was wrong about the children being too excited to sleep tonight,' Cassie said as she came back into the room. 'They were out for the count as soon as their heads touched the pillow.' The fire was throwing out a welcome heat and she found Loveday staring into the flames.

'Okay,' she said, sitting opposite and reaching for the coffee Loveday had made. 'Exactly what *did* happen back there? You still look as white as a ghost.'

Loveday looked up, the shock still clear in her eyes.

'It was a body.'

Cassie stared at her.

'Did . . . ?'

'No . . . Sophie saw nothing. I got her away before she had a chance to look back.'

'But you saw . . . ' She reached for Loveday's hand. 'No wonder you're freaked out.'

Loveday swallowed.

'More than you think, Cassie, you see . . . I think I know who it is.'

* * *

It was well after midnight before she heard Sam's car coming up the drive, and she went to the door to meet him. He put his arms around her.

'Why aren't you in bed?' he asked softly.

'Why do you think?'

'Come on,' he said, leading her back into the warm cottage and sitting her down by the fire. He glanced back to the kitchen. 'I don't suppose you've got any brandy?'

'I think there's some of your malt whisky . . . '

'Even better,' Sam said, slipping off his coat as he went in search of the bottle and some glasses.

He came back with both, handing Loveday a glass containing a generous measure of Glenmorangie.

'Now, sip this slowly,' he said, tilting up

her chin until she looked into his dark, concerned eyes.

'You know I don't drink whisky,' she protested.

'Don't be ridiculous. You're a Scotswoman. You all drink whisky up there. Besides, this one's medicinal.' He grinned down at her. 'Trust me, I'm a doctor.'

Loveday frowned, narrowing her eyes at him, but she took a small mouthful. He was right. She could feel the golden liquid sliding over her throat and spreading comforting warmth around her insides.

Sam took the chair opposite, running a hand through his hair. She could see how tired he was.

'How is Merrick?' she asked quietly.

He frowned.

'Merrick? Why are you asking about him?'

Loveday put down her glass.

'Hasn't he identified the body yet?'

Sam brought his eyebrows together.

'Why would we ask Merrick to identify the body? I doubt if he even knew Billy Travis.'

Loveday jerked forward, staring at him.

'Billy Travis . . . ? You mean it wasn't Cadan back there? But I saw the shoes!'

'Hang on. Can we just reel back a bit? You thought the victim was Merrick's brother? But why?'

'It was the shoes . . . don't you see? He was wearing Cadan's shoes. I recognized them.' The gruesome images were scrolling through her mind. 'At least, I think they were his shoes, the ones he was wearing that day at Morvah. There can't be many expensive hand-stitched Italian jobs like that in Cornwall.'

She looked up and managed a smile. The relief sweeping through her that the body wasn't Cadan's had left her feeling slightly giddy.

'What day at Morvah?' Sam asked.

Loveday quickly outlined her visit to Merrick's house, and her meeting with his brother. She shook her head. 'I don't get it though. Why would Billy Travis be wearing Cadan's shoes?'

'I don't know,' Sam said grimly, throwing back the remains of his Glenmorangie. 'But I intend to find out.'

Loveday's initial relief that the body

308

wasn't Cadan was slowly beginning to ebb away. If he was involved in this it would only add to Merrick's worries. She bit her lip, once again mulling over the possibility that her boss's brother was involved with drugs.

Sam got up to pour himself another whisky. Loveday had hardly touched hers.

He returned and sank back into the chair, loosening his tie.

'Is there anything else I should know?' he said wearily.

'Not really . . . except . . . ' She thought of her visit to Sabine's boutique, and how she had warned her about Cadan.

Sam waited.

'Well, it's nothing, really,' Loveday said. 'Except that I did tell Sabine to be careful about Cadan.'

Sam rolled his eyes.

'I know . . . I know, but I was only trying to help. I suppose you have to speak to her as well now?'

'Possibly.' He wrinkled his brow. 'What's so special about this Sabine anyway that you would want to put her in the magazine?'

'She's unusual, different from anyone I've ever met. I can't imagine what she's doing in Falmouth. With her background I would have thought she'd choose to establish her business in London or Paris.' Loveday shrugged. 'I suppose it takes all kinds.'

'She must have given you some clue about why she's here?'

'She muttered something about the light down here . . . the ambience.'

Sam's head jerked up.

'Is she an artist?'

'She says not, but come to think of it, I did see a collection of picture frames in her stockroom. And there was a very expensive-looking oil painting hanging over her bed. I thought at the time it was an odd place for a picture like that.'

'Why odd?'

'The painting itself was very dark and it was in one of these old-fashioned gilt frames. It didn't suit the rest of the flat at all.'

Sam's brow was wrinkled.

'Could it have been Dutch?'

Loveday gave him a quizzical look.

'Well, probably . . . considering she is. But now that you mention it, it could have been a copy of one of those Old Dutch Masters, although I still can't quite see why she would have it. Sabine didn't strike me as the kind of woman who would settle for anything less than the real thing.'

Loveday's eyes widened as an idea struck her. She looked up at him.

'You don't suppose . . . ?'

★   ★   ★

It was barely seven a.m. when Sam and Will pulled up outside the Tremayne's converted farmhouse. None of the family appeared to be up and about yet. Sam wasn't looking forward to this. Merrick was his friend, and here he was about to accuse his brother of being involved in a murder. He sucked in his cheeks and tried to ignore his discomfort as Will put a finger on the bell.

At the sound of approaching footsteps both men took an involuntary step back as the heavy front door opened. Connie

Bishop eyed Sam with surprise.

'Oh, it's you again, Mr Kitto . . . Inspector. I don't think Mr Tremayne is up yet.'

'We've come to see Cadan again, Connie.' Sam was determined to stay businesslike. 'Can we come in?'

The woman stood aside, indicating they should go into the same front room as before, where a newly-lit fire sparked in the grate. She couldn't hide her concerned frown.

'I'll tell Cadan you're here.'

When she'd gone, Will crossed to the fire, rubbing his hands together and holding them out to the flames.

'Shouldn't one of us have gone up with her? What if he makes a run for it?'

'I hardly think that's likely, Will. Let's just see what he's got to say for himself before we start jumping to any conclusions.'

But it was a possibility he'd considered himself.

When the door opened it wasn't Cadan who appeared, but a rather tousled Merrick, tightening the cord on his dark green dressing-gown.

'What's this all about, Sam?' The

annoyance in his voice was evident. 'What business do you have with Cadan?'

Sam glanced behind him, expecting to see Merrick's brother follow him into the room. But he wasn't there.

'Where is he, Merrick? We need to speak to him.'

Merrick released an exasperated sigh.

'Just tell me what he's done now,' he said wearily. 'Is Cadan in trouble?'

'No, he's not,' said a voice from the stairs.

Cadan, in bare feet and black towelling robe, swept in and glared at Sam.

'You had better have a good reason for this intrusion. I don't appreciate being dragged from my bed at this ungodly hour.'

Sam glanced to Merrick.

'If you don't mind, we'd like to speak to your brother on his own.'

'Well you're not going to,' Merrick said, planting himself firmly in a chair and folding his arms. He fixed Sam with a determined glare. 'If Cadan's done something wrong then I want to know about it.' It was running through his mind that Loveday might had discussed their earlier conversation about Cadan with Sam — but even if she had, would he just turn up like this? No, it had to be something more. Merrick was beginning to feel distinctly uneasy.

Cadan was still eyeing Sam with something close to contempt.

'Well, Inspector . . . we're all waiting,' he said.

Sam met the arrogant stare.

'Will you take a seat, please?'

'I prefer to stand.'

'Sit down, Cadan.' Sam was struggling to keep his irritation under control.

'Do as he says,' Merrick cut in sharply. 'The sooner we can get this over with, the better.'

Cadan went to an armchair and flopped down on it with an exaggerated sigh.

Sam took his time, waiting until he had the man's full attention before saying, 'How well did you know Billy Travis?'

'Who?' Cadan was still trying to sound bored, but Sam had seen the slight stiffening of his upper body.

'Billy Travis,' he repeated. 'His uncle, Jago Tilley, was murdered two weeks ago.'

Out of the corner of his eye he could see Merrick sit forward in his chair.

'Come on, Cadan. It's been in all the papers. You must have read about it.'

Cadan shrugged.

'If you say so.' But his whole body had tensed. He was looking distinctly uncomfortable.

'Mr Travis was found dead last night.' Sam paused to let his words take effect. 'We're treating his death as suspicious.'

'The man was murdered?' Merrick exclaimed. 'Good God, Sam. You can't think that Cadan had anything to do with this?'

Sam swung his head back towards the young man.

'Well, how about it, Cadan? Did you have anything to do with Billy Travis's death?'

Cadan was visibly trembling now. He raised an ashen face to Sam.

'I told you . . . I didn't even know the man.'

Sam and Will exchanged glances as

they watched Cadan squirm. Sam waited, allowing the silence to weigh heavily in the room before going on. 'Can you explain, then, why he was wearing a pair of your shoes?'

Sam could almost see the desperate workings of Cadan's mind.

'Well, tell them, Cadan,' Merrick burst out angrily. 'Did you give this poor man your shoes or not?'

'Merrick,' Sam warned, keeping his voice level. 'It would be best if you left this to — '

But Cadan cut in before he finished his sentence.

'I've told you, I don't even know this man.' He was trying to think fast. How long could he keep this up? He looked away, running the tip of his tongue over his dry lips. The tips of his fingers were tingling.

Sam waited.

'Okay,' Cadan sighed, 'I did give away a pair of old shoes to a stranger. I just didn't know his name.'

Sam frowned. 'Why?'

'Because I felt sorry for him, of course.

It was raining and he only had this pair of old trainers.' He looked up at Sam. 'I just felt sorry for him . . . okay?'

It was one of the lamest excuses Sam had ever heard. He shot Will a glance that signalled he should take up the questioning.

'You said you didn't know Billy Travis.' Will paused, his eyes narrowed. 'Are you in the habit of giving strangers expensive pairs of shoes, Mr Tremayne?'

Cadan shrugged.

'I met him in a pub. We got talking. Maybe I'd had too much to drink . . . I don't know. The shoes were in my car, and I . . . '

Sam gave Merrick an apologetic look.

'Can you get dressed, Cadan? We need you to come down to the station with us.'

Cadan's eyes flew wide and for a second Sam saw the fear there. He should have taken the man in for questioning as soon as they arrived, but for his old friend's sake he'd delayed, hoping the business could be cleared up right here. However, it was obvious that Cadan was more involved than he was admitting.

'Are you arresting me, Inspector?' There was still defiance in the voice.

'You'll be helping us with our enquiries,' Sam responded patiently. 'Of course, if you want us to arrest you . . .'

'Okay.' Cadan jumped up, striding across the room. 'You've made your point.'

Sam nodded for Will to go with him. This time he would take no chances.

Merrick rose wearily from his chair.

'You can't really believe that Cadan had anything to do with this man's death.' He gave Sam a pleading look. 'I know he can be an idiot, but he'd never kill anyone.'

'I'm sorry, Merrick. Cadan's best plan now is to tell us the truth . . . whatever that might be.'

19

Sam had left long before dawn. Loveday knew he was planning to question Cadan that morning. She longed to ring Merrick and tell him she understood what he was going through, but that was the last thing she could do. This was one time when she would definitely have to stay out of Sam's police work.

She went to the sink to rinse out her coffee mug, wondering if Priddy knew about Billy yet. The question was answered minutes later when her mobile rang.

'Can you come over, Loveday?' It was Priddy, and she sounded worried. 'I think I might need your help.'

Loveday didn't waste time questioning her.

'I'll be with you in ten minutes,' she said. She was already reaching for her jacket. She zipped it up as she crossed the road and followed the sea wall at a brisk pace.

The tide was in, and out in the choppy grey waters of the bay the Mount looked bleak and isolated. Priddy must have been watching for her because the cottage door opened before Loveday had even knocked. The old lady's face was pink with fluster as she led Loveday into the familiar warm kitchen.

'Sit yourself down my love, the kettle's just boiled.' Priddy was about to reach for the cups when Loveday took her arm and sat her in the chair by the fire.

'The tea can wait,' she said softly. 'Just tell me what's worrying you.'

Priddy sighed, biting her lip. The cornflower blue eyes met Loveday's.

'Billy's dead. They say he was . . . murdered.'

'Who told you?' Loveday asked gently. The news had obviously upset the old lady.

'Jane and the family were in Penzance last night for that Christmas festival. They saw everything.'

'What?'

'Not the murder. I didn't mean that. They saw Billy's body being taken away and all the police activity. It's not as if I actually liked Billy, but he was Jago's nephew . . . '

Loveday put a comforting arm around Priddy's shoulders.

'I wasn't sure what to do. I should have rung the police as soon as I'd remembered, but they'd have thought what an old fool I was . . . ' Priddy let her words tail off.

Loveday stared at her.

'What is it you've remembered, Priddy?'

'I feel so stupid. I don't know why I didn't think of it before. It's the man who called on Jago . . . the one who wanted to buy the sketch of his mother.'

Loveday felt her pulse quicken.

'Who was this man?'

Priddy shrugged.

'I don't know. It was just something Jago mentioned. He said this antiques dealer was calling at houses in the village offering to buy people's old stuff.'

'How did he know about the sketches?'

'Just the one sketch . . . the one that was in the frame at the time. He spotted it and offered Jago twenty pounds for it.

He didn't know about the others that Jago kept in the back of the frame.'

Loveday's mind was running through all the possibilities this new information fired up. If the man was an antiques dealer, he wouldn't have missed the significance of the signature.

'Did this man come to your door, Priddy?'

'Well, no, that's the thing. I didn't think much about it at the time, but looking back now, it was strange because he'd told Jago that he was calling at all the neighbouring houses.'

'I don't suppose Jago got a name for this man?'

Priddy nodded.

'When Jago refused to sell, the man gave him his card and told him to ring if he changed his mind. He showed it to me.'

Loveday eyed her hopefully but Priddy shook her head.

'You're going to ask me what happened to the card, aren't you? I have no idea, but knowing Jago, he probably binned it.' She chewed on her bottom lip, glancing into the fire. 'I wish I could remember. It was something fancy . . . not a Cornish name.'

Loveday had no idea if this was significant or not, but she knew that Sam had to be told. She said, 'You were right to let me know about this, Priddy. But the people you really need to speak to now are the police.'

'They'll say I should have told them about this man before.'

'I'm sure they will understand,' Loveday said quietly, but she was imagining Sam's annoyance that he hadn't had this information sooner.

Loveday was mulling over what Priddy had told her as she walked back to the cottage. It had all happened months ago, so maybe it was of no significance after all, but even as she considered that, she knew she was wrong. Priddy's caller had to be connected to this business; she just hadn't yet worked out where he fitted it.

She was itching to ring Sam, but this had to come from Priddy. All the same, she would check with him in an hour or so to make sure she had called.

She turned into the drive, hoping she could slip into the cottage without being noticed. As much as she loved Cassie, this was not the time for a cosy chat. She had some thinking to do.

Closing the back door quietly behind her, Loveday slipped off her jacket and hung it on the door before going off to find her notebook. Writing things down always helped to clear her mind.

She made a list of everyone who was in any way connected to the murders. Priddy's name was at the top because she had discovered Jago's body. She jotted down Billy Travis, who had believed he would inherit his uncle's cottage. And then there was Ray Penrose of the Newlyyn Fishermen's Federation . . . She chewed the end of her pen. Penrose would have known the cottage would come to his organization. She had no idea how financially secure it was, but if it was in need of funds then perhaps the man also had a motive for bringing on Jago's death?

There was Cadan, of course, which also meant she should add his girlfriend

Sabine's name to the list.

She sat back, running her eyes down what she had written. Somewhere in the back of her mind, she remembered Sam had mentioned questioning an art dealer in St Ives.

She jotted down the words and stared at them. 'Art dealer' wasn't a million miles away from 'antiques dealer', and it wasn't outside the realm of possibility that Billy had told the man about Jago's sketches. He could have been the one Jago told Priddy about. Loveday's list had come full circle back to Priddy, who had recalled that the man had a fancy name.

She frowned, staring at the page. It was just a list of names, and yet she was sure that somehow they all fitted into the same puzzle.

Her mobile phone trilled and she reached for it, her pulse quickening when she saw Merrick's name. She'd been itching to call him all morning, but what could she say? She had no idea when Sam had planned to call on Cadan, and she could have stirred up a hornets' nest if she'd jumped the gun and asked Merrick

325

about it. But he'd rung her.

'Merrick! Is everything all right?' Such a ridiculous thing to ask when she knew it almost certainly was not.

'Sam's taken Cadan in for questioning,' Merrick said abruptly. 'He thinks he had something to with that poor devil who was murdered in Penzance.'

A chill ran through Loveday as the image of Billy Travis's body, dumped in the bushes where his killer had dragged him, leapt into her mind again. Could Cadan really have been responsible for that? He was a rogue, certainly — and selfish and inconsiderate — but a killer? She shook her head. It wasn't possible.

'Sam thinks he murdered the man.' Merrick's voice was spiked with misery.

Loveday cleared her throat.

'I'm sure he doesn't think that, Merrick. You know how these investigations work. Questioning Cadan will be a routine thing, just another line of enquiry.'

'He was wearing Cadan's shoes, Loveday.'

She bit her lip. Should she have kept her mouth shut about those shoes? But how could she? If Cadan was involved in Billy's murder, then the truth would have to come out. She just wished she could protect Merrick, and their frail old father, from the hurt. She took a deep breath.

'I know about the shoes, Merrick. I was the one who found the body.'

'What!'

She began to repeat herself, but Merrick jumped in. 'Did I hear right? It was you who found the body?'

'More than that, I'm afraid. You see, I recognized the shoes the man was wearing. They were pretty distinctive.' She paused. 'And the last time I saw them, Cadan was wearing them. So you see, Merrick, it's all my fault that he's being questioned by the police.'

The silence that followed made her wonder if he'd heard what she'd said. She wanted to ask how Merrick's brother had known Billy Travis, but further probing on her part now could only make matters worse.

As though he had read her thoughts, Merrick suddenly said, 'Cadan didn't kill this man. I'd stake my life on that.' He sighed. 'But he did lie to Sam. He told him he'd met the man in a pub and felt sorry for him so he gave him the shoes from the boot of his car.'

This image of a caring Cadan was hard to swallow. Try as she might, Loveday couldn't picture Cadan just handing over a pair of expensive Italian leather shoes, not unless he was forced into it.

'And then there's this business about the drugs,' Merrick continued. 'If my brother has been taking drugs, then who knows what he could be capable of?'

'You don't know that Cadan is taking drugs, Merrick.' She paused. 'I think we should keep an open mind about this, at least until we know more. One thing you can be certain of, though, is that Sam will not be charging Cadan with anything, not without evidence, and the fact that Billy Travis was wearing your brother's shoes is not evidence.'

Merrick gave a little laugh.

'Always the voice of reason, Loveday.'

'Just stating the facts, that's all, Merrick.'

The call ended with Merrick's promise

to update her about any new developments. She sat there for a moment wondering if she should ring Sam and tip him off about what Priddy had told her. The antiques dealer with the fancy name, who had offered to buy Jago's sketch of his mother, could be the man they were looking for.

Her hand hovered over the phone, and then a voice in her head warned her about interfering again. She would call on Priddy later just to check that she had contacted the police, and only if she hadn't would she tell Sam about Jago's caller.

* * *

Will looked up, a phone clamped to his ear, as Sam walked into the CID room.

'I think we've found Paxton-Quinn, boss,' he said.

Sam tried not to shudder. He knew what was coming. 'Where is he?'

The detective winced as he met his superior officer's eyes. 'Just round the corner, actually.' He paused. 'His body got tangled up on a boat anchor near the steps at the ferry terminal. DC Fox is down there.'

Sam was already on his way. 'Come on, Will,' he called over his shoulder. 'You too, Malcolm.'

It took them less than three minutes to hurry down, skirt the roundabout, and cross the Malpas Road to the ferry platform used by the boats that brought passengers from Falmouth.

A police vehicle was already at the scene, and Sam could see Amanda talking to a middle-aged, grey-haired man by the open door of his car.

The three officers stared down at the mud-covered body of Zachariah Paxton-Quinn. Sam sighed. This was his fault. He should have taken the man in for questioning in the first place. If he hadn't been given the chance to take off, he might still be alive.

'Get the troops out, Will,' he instructed. 'We need forensics and Dr Bartholomew out here.' His eyes wandered upstream to where he could see channels of water beginning to creep towards them. 'And tell them to make it quick. We're fighting the tide again here.'

He walked over to the two uniformed officers who were standing by their vehicle. The younger one was looking distinctly green.

'Who found the body?' he asked.

The older officer pointed to the man Amanda was interviewing.

'He lives up the road there, in Malpas. He was on his way to Tesco to buy his Sunday paper, and had stopped to let the dog out of the car. That's when he saw it. He's still pretty shocked. We've got his name and address, but we knew you would want to speak to him.'

'Okay, get this area taped off as best you can,' he ordered, glancing up at the small crowd that had started to gather. 'And keep those people well away.'

He turned to Will Tregellis and Malcolm Carter. 'I want you two to get started knocking on a few doors.' He glanced around all the buildings he could see. 'I want everyone with access to any of those windows that overlook the site questioned.'

The two officers exchanged a look.

'Now, please,' Sam said. 'Somebody must have seen something.'

It was another fifteen minutes before the Home Office pathologist's big green BMW screeched to a halt on the road a few feet away.

'We can't go on meeting like this, Sam,' Dr Bartholomew puffed past him.

The Scene of Crime team had arrived moments earlier and had begun setting up their equipment to record every possible scrap of evidence.

Dr Bartholomew rose from his knees and mopped his forehead with a white handkerchief.

'Pointless, in my mind,' he said. 'This poor chap has undoubtedly been dumped here at high tide, which means sometime during night, when it would have been dark.'

'You don't think it's a suicide then?' Sam asked.

'Not unless he bashed himself on the back of the head first.'

Sam blew out his cheeks and ran a hand over his head. 'You're telling me he was murdered, Robert?'

'Well, I can't give you a definite until I get him on the slab; but I'd say yes, you've got yourself another murder.'

★　★　★

Sam hadn't called, which meant he was busy. Loveday knew better than to interrupt him. She wasn't quite sure why she was driving to Falmouth on such a miserable Sunday afternoon. The chances of finding Sabine De Fries at home seemed remote — unless, of course, she had opened the boutique on the chance of some last-minute Christmas business.

She wasn't looking forward to breaking the news that Cadan was being questioned by the police; but, as his girlfriend, Sabine had a right to know. At the very least, she deserved the chance to offer her support.

The roads were quiet as she turned off the roundabout and drove down the hill into Falmouth. Loveday was surprised to see that quite a number of shops on the narrow cobbled street were open for business. But Sabine's boutique was not one of them. The little shop was in darkness as Loveday motored past and turned down into the waterside car park she had used before.

Finding a parking space this time was no problem. As she walked back up to the street, a movement down by the rear of the shops caught her eye. They all backed on to the harbour, and her earlier thought that some of the properties would have a landing area for a boat had been right.

She went to the rail and moved her gaze slowly along the row of back doors. She couldn't detect any movement now.

Sabine's apartment was easy to spot with its white balcony. Directly below it was a wooden landing from which steps descended to a small blue and white tender.

Loveday's eye was again drawn to the back door of the shop, which she estimated must be accessed from the stockroom. As she watched, the door opened and Sabine appeared carrying what looked like a fuel can. She went on watching as Sabine climbed on board and disappeared into the cabin.

Loveday hoped the woman was not about to motor off somewhere. But seconds later she had reappeared, hopped back onto the jetty, and marched back up to the shop.

Loveday hurried up the slope to the street. She had no idea why her pulse had quickened. She only wanted to talk to Sabine. She stood outside the boutique door looking for a bell, but there didn't appear to be one. She was already regretting her decision to come here.

It had been her who had warned Sabine about Cadan in the first place. If she had taken that on board she might already have finished with him. She had no reason to believe that Sabine would want to offer Cadan any support, and perhaps he didn't deserve it. Loveday just couldn't shift the uncomfortable feeling that she was in some way responsible for what was happening to him. If she could make amends by enlisting Sabine's help then at least she would feel better.

She had been about to turn away when the door opened and Sabine, glamorous as ever in a pale cashmere coat, rushed out and almost careered into her. The woman's green eyes flew wide open.

'Loveday! What are you doing here?'

'I . . . hmm.' Loveday shuffled her feet, not quite sure what to say. 'I was passing, and I thought . . . but you're off out.' She waved a dismissive hand. 'It was nothing important.'

Sabine caught Loveday's glance along the street. Most of the other shops were open and appeared to be doing brisk business in last minute Christmas sales.

'I needed some time off, and Francine likes to spend Sundays with her family,' she said quickly.

'It's your boutique, Sabine. You can close it whenever you like.'

The sage eyes narrowed as though the woman was unsure what to do. She flashed a dazzling smile at Loveday.

'I was only planning some window-shopping, but it can keep. Come up to the apartment for some coffee.'

Wherever Sabine had been hurrying off to, Loveday was sure it was not a window-shopping expedition. Had Cadan already been in touch? Had Sabine been on her way to the police station in Truro?

Loveday would have been quite happy to walk away a moment ago, but now she was intrigued. She followed the waft of Sabine's musky scent through the darkened shop and into the stockroom, and then upstairs to the apartment.

'Make yourself at home,' Sabine called, discarding the expensive coat over the arm of a chair as she disappeared into the kitchen.

Loveday heard the chink of cups. She wandered over to the French windows. It had started to rain and the day outside was dark and gloomy. She glanced down, stretching on tiptoes to see if she could spot the boat Sabine had carried fuel to, but it was directly below the balcony and as such out of sight.

'Not quite so glamorous in this weather, is it?'

Loveday spun round. She hadn't heard Sabine's approach and wondered how long she had been watching her.

'What were you looking for just now?' The cat's eyes narrowed again and Loveday swallowed, feeling like a naughty child who had just been caught stealing fruit from someone else's apple tree.

'I was just ... the boats ... ' she began.

Sabine had stepped closer.

'This wasn't a spur-of-the-moment visit was it, Loveday? Exactly what are you doing here?'

20

Loveday put up her hands in a placating gesture. She didn't like this new glint of venom in the woman's cold stare.

She swallowed. 'Okay, I was planning to choose my moment, but now is as good a time as any.'

Sabine was still glaring at her.

'It's Cadan.'

The woman's eyes narrowed a fraction, but she said nothing, so Loveday continued.

'The police have taken him in for questioning.'

If she'd expected concern, distress even, she was disappointed. The accusing stares merely hardened. But there was more. For a second Loveday thought she'd caught a flash of panic.

'Questioning about what?' Sabine said coldly.

They were still facing each other, but the confrontational stance had gone.

'A man's body was found in Penzance

last night. The police are treating it as murder.'

Sabine flinched.

'Cadan murdered someone?' She was pacing the room now. It wasn't the reaction Loveday had expected.

'I didn't say that, Sabine. I'm sure his connection with this man can be explained.'

'There's a connection?'

Loveday frowned.

'Apparently Cadan gave this man his shoes. They were on his body when . . . '

Sabine wheeled round.

'It sounds pretty conclusive to me. Do the police know about Cadan's gambling problem? Maybe this man was blackmailing him.'

Loveday stared at her. Given that the woman was supposed to be in love with Cadan, the least she'd been expecting was indignant outrage on his behalf, but Sabine seemed intent on building a case against him.

'I bought those shoes for him, you know,' she muttered. 'How could he be so ungrateful?'

Loveday was struggling to make sense

of what she was hearing. Hadn't this woman tried to bail Cadan out of his debt problems? At least, that was the story Cassie's friends had heard. If that was true, then why was she suddenly turning against him?

Loveday took a deep breath.

'I take it you're not going to help him, then.'

Sabine fixed her with an amused stare.

'This has nothing to do with me.'

Loveday would be the first to admit that Cadan Tremayne had his faults, but he was Merrick's brother, and he deserved better than this.

'Forget the coffee, Sabine. I won't be staying.' Out of the corner of her eye as she left the room, she caught a smile twitch at the edge of Sabine's mouth.

'I can let myself out,' she called back as she ran down the stairs. But when she reached the front door, she stopped. Something wasn't right. Sabine had said she'd bought the shoes Cadan gave to Billy. Loveday chewed on her bottom lip. How did Sabine know which shoes?

She opened the door but didn't go out.

Slamming it with force, she stepped back into the shadows of the shop. The window display prevented much light from the outside street penetrating the interior, but there was enough to stop Loveday from bumping into things.

She had no idea why she was behaving in such a furtive way, or what she would do if Sabine discovered her. She could hear the woman's quick step as she moved around upstairs.

Loveday was hoping Sabine would leave and head off to wherever she had been going earlier, so she could have a snoop around, but that didn't seem to be happening. She could hear the soft murmur of Sabine's voice. She was speaking to someone on the phone. Loveday's heart stopped. She was coming down the stairs!

Loveday cast a desperate glance around, deciding her best option was to crouch down behind the counter. She could hear Sabine in the back room now. She was still talking on the phone. Heart pumping, she strained to listen, but could catch only snatches of the conversation — ' . . . paintings . . . boat . . . last time.' It wasn't difficult to piece together their meaning.

It was all beginning to make sense.

She thought back to the painting she had glimpsed in Sabine's bedroom. She had only seen it for a second, but she was sure now that it hadn't been a copy of a Dutch Master. It hadn't been dark enough for that, but there had been something familiar about it.

Loveday tried to recall her conversation with Rebecca Monteith at the Penzance gallery. They had strolled around the paintings as she described the works of Walter Langley, Stanhope Forbes, Dame Laura Knight and their contemporaries.

There was a connection here, she was sure of it. She just hadn't worked it all out yet.

Her heart gave a sudden lurch. The thought that flashed into her head was too ridiculous to give serious consideration to, and yet . . .

She could still hear Sabine moving around the stockroom, but the telephone conversation appeared to have finished.

Loveday was still crouched down behind the counter, but painful cramps were beginning to travel up her legs. She stood up to flex her stiffened muscles, just as her phone let out a noisy trill. Diving into her pocket, she fumbled frantically to switch the thing off, but it was too late.

Sabine had come in, flicked on the boutique lights and was staring furiously at her.

For a second, neither of them spoke; and then, deciding attack would be her best defence, Loveday narrowed her eyes at the woman.

'I know everything,' she said.

She hadn't noticed the knife the woman held down by her side, but as Sabine drew it up and pointed it at Loveday, the blade glinted.

'You shouldn't have interfered, Loveday. That was your big mistake.' Sabine moved forward, snapping closed the window blind. 'I even liked you.'

Loveday stared at her as the realization dawned.

'It was you who killed Billy.' She shook her head. 'But why . . . what had he done to you?'

Sabine sighed.

'He knew about the old man. The brainless idiot thought he could blackmail me.'

Loveday's eyes widened.

'The old man? Do you mean Jago?' Her voice was rising in disbelief. 'You killed Jago?'

'I didn't mean to . . . it was his own fault. I'd gone round there several times before — even offered him money — but he wouldn't part with the sketches.'

'And for that you beat a poor old man to death?' Loveday couldn't believe what she was hearing.

'He fell down the stairs. It was an accident,' Sabine said.

'He was beaten with a poker,' Loveday spat back.

'Well . . . yes. I couldn't just leave him lying there staring up at me with those accusing eyes. I had to put him out of his misery.'

Loveday was shaking with rage.

'How did you even get into Jago's cottage? There were no signs of a break-in.'

Sabine gave Loveday an indignant stare.

'Billy gave me a key, of course. I don't

break into people's houses. What do you think I — '

'But it was all for nothing anyway,' Loveday interrupted, 'because you didn't get the sketches, did you?'

'No, I didn't,' Sabine said, narrowing her eyes at Loveday. 'That was you, interfering again. Why didn't you leave them in your cottage? You don't know how much trouble you've caused me.' Her voice was threatening.

Loveday's mouth dropped open.

'It was you who ransacked my cottage?' She raised a hand to lash out at her, but Sabine caught her wrist, twisting it until Loveday flinched at the pain.

'Were you planning to make Cadan the scapegoat for the old man's murder too?' Her words came out in a strangled yelp. 'You didn't really believe you would get away with it, did you?'

And then a thought struck her. 'This is all about your obsession with art, isn't it? Merrick's house wasn't burgled at all, was it? It was you who made Cadan steal that picture from his father.'

She could still feel the point of the

knife in her back, but she wasn't going to stop now. 'You killed two people for a few pictures?' Loveday's voice was incredulous.

The hand holding the knife relaxed. 'But they weren't just any pictures. They were Cornish artists . . . previously unknown sketches by Walter Langley, and the two Alfred Wallis pictures.'

'Two?' Loveday jumped in.

Sabine was still brandishing the knife, but she had turned Loveday to face her. 'Cadan can be very accommodating when he tries,' she said sweetly.

'I didn't know about the other painting. Who did Cadan steal that one from?'

'Someone who didn't deserve to have it in the first place. I relieved him of it, that's all.'

Her voice had become reflective, and she was beginning to speak as though she'd forgotten Loveday was there. 'I lost pretty heavily on the tables one night, and the owner of the casino came to seek me out. He assumed I'd be vulnerable . . . in his debt. He didn't know it was all part of the plan.

'Within the week, Rupe Caine had

347

moved me into his ridiculously ostentatious house on the outskirts of Plymouth. The stuff he put on his walls was gross, and I told him so. That's when he agreed to trust me to purchase his works of art. He had money, and I enjoyed spending it for him.'

She was moving about the boutique now, waving the knife to emphasize what she was saying. Loveday's eyes followed her around the room. She was poised . . . waiting for her chance to pounce on Sabine.

'That's when I discovered the Cornish painters.' She put her hand on her throat. 'I had no idea artists down here were creating work like this. It was magical. I had to have a collection of their paintings and sketches.'

She wheeled round, fixing Loveday with a wild look. 'That's what I do, you see. I collect works of art.' She moved her face closer to Loveday's. 'You can understand that, can't you?'

Loveday sneered at her. 'That flat upstairs isn't big enough to display any paintings.'

Sabine's green eyes glinted. 'Not here. You don't imagine I keep my treasures in this place? The cellar of my home in France is my gallery.' She waved the knife around again. 'This is just a cover for my real work.'

'And what's that?' Loveday asked shakily, realizing the woman was probably completely mad.

'I'm rescuing treasures, saving these works of art for posterity.'

'After you've stolen them,' Loveday muttered under her breath.

'After I've released them,' Sabine said sharply, prodding the knife into Loveday's side. 'We're going for a little trip now.'

She pushed Loveday towards the storeroom door. Loveday could feel the point of the knife at her back again as she was forced across the room. The shop's rear door was thrown open and she felt a rush of icy night air sting her face as she was pushed, stumbling, into the darkness.

They were making for the tender. Away up on the right, Loveday could see the lights of the car park, where she had left the Clio less than an hour before. She supposed most of the shops would be closed now; most people would have gone home. The thought made her feel bleaker than ever.

Sabine was shoving her down the wooden steps to the little landing where the boat was tied up. The lighting was poor, and twice she had to grab the rickety metal rail to stop herself plunging into the murky water below.

The boat rocked alarmingly as Loveday stepped aboard, and again she had to make a grab for the side to steady herself.

'Where are we going?' she yelled back, the wind snatching at every word as she shouted.

'You'll see,' Sabine barked, following her onto the boat.

The lights of the harbour twinkled ahead, but out in the black waters of Carrick Roads no vessels seemed to be moving. Loveday shivered. She could hear the waves slapping against the side of the boat.

A sudden gust of wind caught the bow, tugging the boat violently at its mooring. Both women lurched forward. Loveday took her chance, making a grab for the knife, but Sabine lashed out at her, slicing a gash on her hand. Loveday let out a yelp and jumped back, catching her foot on the planking and ending up sprawled across the wet deck.

She hadn't realized she had struck her head until she felt the warm blood tricking down her face.

'Get up,' Sabine screamed, giving Loveday a kick. The knife was at her throat now. 'And never try anything like that again.'

Loveday considered feigning unconsciousness — but if she did that, what was to stop Sabine from taking the boat out into deep water and dumping her over the side? She struggled to her feet, fighting back tears. She had no intention of letting this crazy woman see her weakness.

'Why are you doing this?' She glared up at her, trying to keep her voice steady.

'You should have kept out of my business,' Sabine growled. 'If you hadn't poked your nose in then I would have gone away, and you would never have heard from me again.'

'You murdered two people, Sabine.'

Loveday's voice was rising. 'Have you no conscience?'

'You don't know the half of it.' Sabine's smile was chilling, and Loveday was again reminded she was dealing with a mad woman. 'It's art that's important. People who don't appreciate real art shouldn't be allowed to have it.'

Loveday touched her forehead and her fingers came away wet. The pain in her head was making her feel nauseous.

'You're a thief and a murderer, Sabine, and you can dress it up any way you like. You kill people . . . and steal from them.'

'I don't steal . . . I relieve the ignorant of what they don't understand.'

'There's a difference?'

'Well, of course there is,' Sabine snapped. 'I revere true artists. I preserve their work.'

All the time she spoke she was moving about the boat, making it ready to leave, but she never took her sights off Loveday.

Loveday eyed the knife.

'I would have thought there were enough Grand Masters in the Netherlands to satisfy any art collector. Why come to Cornwall?'

Sabine stared at her, the knife poised.

'For the Newlyn artists, of course — and the others. I thought you would have realized that. The old man's sketches would have been a real prize . . . Langley sketches that had never been seen in public before. What a treasure they would have been.' She glanced back to the cabin where she had stashed a black bin bag. 'I'll have to be satisfied with what I already have.'

'You've got paintings by some of the Newlyn artists?' Loveday's voice was disbelieving.

Sabine nodded, and gave a dreamy smile. 'Stanhope and Elizabeth Forbes, Bramley, the Knights, Garstin . . . and Langley, of course. I have them all.'

Either the woman was mad or she had managed to pull off one the biggest art heists Cornwall had ever known. So why hadn't she heard about it?

'Are you saying there are works of art in the bin bag back there?'

'Don't worry,' Sabine said airily. 'They will receive the reverence they deserve when I get them home.'

'You mean to Amsterdam?'

'No, I mean *home*.' She waved the knife under Loveday's nose. 'You're asking too many questions. Now grab that fuel can from the cabin and fill the tank.'

Loveday had been wondering why Sabine hadn't immediately fired up the engine and taken off, now she knew. The boat's fuel tank was empty. The woman had probably been trying to work out these past few minutes how to deal with the situation, while keeping Loveday at bay with the knife.

'Well? What are you waiting for? I said *move*.'

Loveday scrambled into the cabin.

'I can't find any fuel can. Where is it?'

'At the back . . . on the left, there.'

Loveday knew exactly where it was. This could be her last chance.

'It's not here,' she insisted. 'There's no fuel can in here.'

Sabine gave a frustrated grunt. The boat rocked as she stepped into the cabin.

Loveday made her move. In one sharp effort, she jabbed her elbow back, connecting with Sabine's stomach. The woman let out a yelp and doubled up in pain. The knife clattered to the floor of the cabin and Loveday made a grab for it, gathering all her strength to hurl it over the side.

Pushing the whimpering woman aside, she scrambled back up the boat, feeling for the rope she'd spotted earlier. The vessel continued to rock violently as she turned back. Grabbing the woman's arms she yanked them behind her back, and ignoring her cries of pain, lashed her wrists together as tightly as she could. Then she tied the loose ends of the rope to the seat before slumping back exhausted against the side of the boat.

'I'll kill you for this,' Sabine spat, but her venom no longer worried Loveday.

'It's over, Sabine,' she said wearily. 'It's all over.'

It had begun to sleet. Loveday ran a hand over her wet hair and then reached for her phone before realizing that Sabine had grabbed it earlier. It was now somewhere at the bottom of Falmouth Harbour.

She sat for a moment, not sure what to do. Her head was really beginning to hurt now. She was struggling to stand up when she heard the feet pounding towards her.

Sam was the first to reach her, and then Will and Amanda. More officers were storming towards them from the back door of Sabine's boutique.

Sam's arms came around her as he stroked her hair. 'Thank God you're all right, my darling,' he was saying.

From somewhere far off she could hear Amanda's voice. 'We need an ambulance down here. NOW!'

That's when everything started to sway, and the whole world went black.

★　★　★

Loveday felt a fraud as they led her away to the ambulance. 'It was only a faint,' she protested. 'I'm fine now, really I am.' But her voice was unsteady.

Sam shook his head as he climbed into the ambulance after her. 'There's a nasty gash on your head, and your hand's bleeding. Of course you're not fine, Loveday.'

She opened her mouth to remonstrate,

but he put a finger to her lips, and then kissed her.

Loveday felt the tears trickle down her cheeks. He brushed them away, gently lifting the strands of dark hair from her face as the ambulance set off for the local Minor Injuries Unit.

'How did you know where to find me, Sam?' she said shakily.

'I didn't. It was Sabine we were after. I had no idea you were here.'

He tucked a blanket around her shoulders.

'We got lucky,' he said. 'An old reprobate we interviewed in Hale when we were trying to find Paxton-Quinn told us his daughter knew about a mysterious girlfriend. We had to wait until she returned from Paris to discover who that was.'

'And she told you it was Sabine De Fries,' Loveday said, the penny dropping.

'Correct,' Sam said, as the ambulance drew to a halt outside the MIU. He reached forward and touched Loveday's cheek. 'And I'll never stop being grateful to her.'

21

Every seat on the plane was occupied as they raced down the runway at Newquay Airport on Christmas Eve.

Normally when Loveday travelled home to Scotland she would drive, breaking her journey with an overnight stop in York. This was a much more civilized way to make the trip.

But she still reached for Sam's hand as the engines powered up, and the aircraft lifted from the ground.

'Don't tell me you're afraid of flying?' he said.

'Just this taking off bit.' She slid him a sheepish grin. 'A glass of something usually does the trick.'

The seatbelt signs went off, and the rumble of wheels could be heard as two members of cabin crew began dispensing drinks from a trolley.

Ten minutes later, as Loveday sipped her Chardonnay and Sam was tipping the second miniature of Glenlivet into his plastic glass, she turned to him.

'So . . . Cadan's off the hook,' she said.

Sam pursed his lips. 'I wouldn't say that. There's still the small matter of those two Wallis pictures he stole.'

'But I thought they were recovered, along with the rest of Sabine's collection.'

'They were, and there's a possibility that both his father and Rupe Caine will drop the charges.

'He's told us everything . . . well, everything he knew. I don't doubt that he was taken in by a very persuasive woman.'

Loveday sighed, and put down her wine.

'Sabine fooled me too. I still can't believe how devious she was.'

Sam grimaced, remembering the interview at Truro police headquarters. The woman had freely admitted everything. It should have been a satisfactory conclusion to the case, but it wasn't. Sabine De Fries seemed completely oblivious to the fact that she had done anything wrong.

She had killed Jago, Billy and Paxton-Quinn, and showed no remorse. And in the end it had been all for nothing.

The paintings that her accomplice, Zachariah Paxton-Quinn, had passed to her were copies. The originals were all still back where they belonged — with their owners. She had been well and truly double-crossed.

Sam sat back, his eyes on Loveday's face. 'The talented, if dishonest, artist Quinn had found to reproduce the pictures did a good job. The paintings were masterpieces of deception. Well, they had to be, to fool Sabine.'

Loveday shook her head. 'I still can't quite believe all this.'

I'm not surprised,' Sam said. 'But the fact is that Paxton-Quinn did set up those break-ins at small galleries all over the South West to switch the paintings. None of the originals were ever stolen, so the gallery owners just assumed it had been a burglary gone wrong. It sufficed that Sabine believed it had happened. She'd believed she owned a collection of masterpieces when all the time the pictures were counterfeit.'

He smiled. 'She cared about that, all right. She never stopped ranting about it back at the station to anyone who would listen.'

Loveday took another sip of her wine and pressed her lips together.

'But if she didn't know that Quinn had been passing her fakes, why did she kill him?'

Sam glanced out as the snow-topped mountains of the Highlands came into view. 'Quinn was panicking. Sabine thought he was going to spill the beans about their little operation, and she couldn't allow that to happen.'

Loveday shook her head. 'Poor man.' She ran a finger around the rim of her glass. 'There's something I still don't understand. You said Cadan hadn't actually given his shoes to Billy Travis, so why was he wearing them?'

'It was Sabine who did that,' Sam said. 'It wasn't difficult, given that Cadan often stayed overnight at her flat in Falmouth and kept some of his clothes there.

'He realized at once that it must have been her who had killed Billy, but he was still obsessed with her.' He shook his head. 'He was trying to cover for her by claiming that it was him who had given Billy the shoes.'

'What about his gambling debt?' Loveday asked. 'Was that a fantasy too?'

Sam sighed.

'Not exactly. He did apparently owe a great deal of money to the casino in Plymouth. What Merrick told you about Rupe Caine wanting Cadan to smuggle drugs in from the Continent was true. He was trying to force Cadan's hand by telling him he would wipe the debt clean if he did what he was told.

'Fortunately Cadan came to his senses before he'd got involved. But he had seriously considered it.'

Loveday nodded.

'So he's still left with the gambling debt. Poor Merrick, he's soft enough about his brother to cough up for it.'

'There is no gambling debt. Caine was running a crooked establishment. The tables had been fixed so that none of the customers ever won substantial amounts of cash. They did, however, tend to lose pretty heavily.'

'Well, at least Merrick will be relieved,' she said. 'I'm beginning to suspect he's secretly quite fond of his wayward brother.'

'He might well be, but he's still laying down the law about Cadan's future behaviour. He's told him that he must mend his ways if he wants to go on living at Morvah, and since Cadan doesn't have anywhere else to go — if he escapes prison, that is — I guess he has no choice.'

Loveday sighed.

'I won't hold my breath over that one.'

'We'll see,' Sam said. 'But I think that young man has had a serious fright. He won't be stepping back out of line in a hurry.' He gave Loveday a crooked grin. 'Well . . . not for while, anyway.'

Loveday rested her head against the seat and glanced down at the familiar Scottish peaks. They would soon be touching down at Inverness. She felt a little flurry of excitement. Turning back to Sam, she studied his handsome profile, wondering what he would make of her slightly unconventional family. And then she frowned.

'Are you sure you want to do this?' she said.

'What, Christmas in the Highlands? Why wouldn't I?' His mouth twitched into a grin. 'Besides . . . I have to meet your folks sometime.'

'They'll be quite busy,' she said quickly. 'The pub is manic at this time of year, so don't expect to be waited on.'

Sam put a finger under her chin and turned her head, forcing her to look at him.

'You're not sorry you invited me, are you, Loveday?'

'Of course not . . . it's just . . . ' She swallowed. 'Well, Inverness isn't Cornwall.' She took his hand. 'I so want you to enjoy this Christmas, Sam.'

Now that the case had been more or less wrapped up, and Sabine De Fries had been charged with all three murders, Loveday worried that Sam's mood might start to plummet again. She could only imagine how frustrating it must be for him, knowing that another man was spoiling his kids this Christmas. She would have to take very good care of him.

Sam was thinking his own thoughts. He was aware that Loveday's invitation to spend the holiday with her family had been a last minute decision. As far as he knew she'd always planned to come up here on her own. He hoped she wasn't regretting it.

He'd been raging when Victoria announced that her new man was treating the whole family to a holiday in Florida. It should have been him doing that. But over the past week he'd felt his mood mellowing. Jack and Maddie Skyped him every day, and they would be home in three more days. It wasn't such a big deal any more.

The trip to Scotland was Loveday's attempt to stop him from brooding, and he loved her for it. She had gone to a lot of trouble to make him happy. It felt good to have someone care about him that much.

He turned back to her and found the dark blue eyes were studying him.

'What's up?'

She shrugged.

'Nothing's up.' She glanced out of the window. He waited.

'I just hope you like my parents, Sam, that's all.'

'Are they aliens?'

She picked up her magazine and playfully whacked it at him.

'Mum and Dad are not aliens, they're

just not your average fifty-somethings.'

He lifted an eyebrow.

'Mum likes to help people, you know
. . . to get involved. Don't get me wrong,
she doesn't pry, she just has everybody's
interests at heart. Dad tries to keep his
head down, but at the end of the day he
just kind of goes along with it. They're
actually very happy together.'

She grimaced, meeting his amused stare.
'You might find Mum asks a lot of questions, so just don't take it the wrong way.'

Sam eyed her from under his brow.

'Are you saying your mother is an
interfering woman?'

'I never said that.'

Sam laughed, shaking his head.

'What?' she said.

'Nothing,' he said, still laughing.
'Nothing at all . . . '

We do hope that you have enjoyed reading this large print book.

Did you know that all of our titles are available for purchase?

We publish a wide range of high quality large print books including:
Romances, Mysteries, Classics
General Fiction
Non Fiction and Westerns

Special interest titles available in large print are:
The Little Oxford Dictionary
Music Book, Song Book
Hymn Book, Service Book

Also available from us courtesy of Oxford University Press:
Young Readers' Dictionary
(large print edition)
Young Readers' Thesaurus
(large print edition)

For further information or a free brochure, please contact us at:
Ulverscroft Large Print Books Ltd.,
The Green, Bradgate Road, Anstey,
Leicester, LE7 7FU, England.
Tel: (00 44) **0116 236 4325**
Fax: (00 44) **0116 234 0205**

THE WITCHES' MOON

Gerald Verner

Mr. Dench left his house on a wet September night to post a letter at a nearby pillar-box — and disappeared. A fortnight later his dead body was found in a tunnel a few miles away. He had been brutally murdered. Called in to investigate, Superintendent Robert Budd soon realizes that Dench hadn't planned to disappear. But it's not until he finds the secret of the fireman's helmet, the poetic pickpocket, and the Witches' Moon that he discovers why Mr. Dench — and several other people — have been murdered . . .

TILL THE DAY I DIE

V. J. Banis

Shot at point-blank range while trying to prevent the kidnapping of her daughter Becky, book editor Catherine Desmond has a mysterious near-death experience. When she recovers, she learns that Becky has been murdered by a gang of child abusers, who are still active and being hunted by the police. To her dismay, she finds herself linked psychically with Becky's killer — and he begins shadowing her as well. An ethereal cat-and-mouse game ensues, with life — and death — hanging in the balance . . .